A CHILD OF HER OWN

JULIAN PEARCE

Contents

For Angela with love and appreciation for
months of patience and counsel.

Chapter 1

Initiations Of Youth

Jack had got to know Susie in the way salesmen make a point of getting to know the secretaries of their clients; the path for achieving a close client relationship and thereby a good sales record, he had learned, lay through the secretary. She was Jack's trusted collaborator, his inside representative subtly to push his interests behind closed doors. Susie's boss, James Derby, was the advertising manager and print buyer for Luxus Travel, and whilst Jack's interests lay almost entirely in maintaining the numerous print contracts for their travel brochures, James's interest was in laying Susie - behind closed doors. As a bubbly young nymphomaniac Susie's collaborations were happily divided: Jack got the contracts, James got Susie, and Susie got laid. Not a conventional *ménage a trios* perhaps, but pragmatic in its application.

As a young man of twenty four Jack Strange was well

blessed; he had all the advantages of a privileged upbringing, coupled with innate attributes beneficial for success in the pool of commerce in which he swam. Of medium height, slim, fair, good looking, quick witted and well dressed, he possessed a strong will to achieve concealed under a boyish charm. It had not been Jack's choice to become a salesman – or sales representative as those so employed preferred – he had needed a job, and the only job offered was in sales: selling advertising space in women's magazines. On leaving school he had not gone to university, not as a matter of his deliberation, but rather more on the basis of his complete lack of any academic ability to pass the requisite exams. His romantic aspiration had been to go to live in Paris, to study fine art at Les Beaux Arts, to be an artist, to smoke Gaullois, drink Pastis, perfect his French under the tutelage (or on top of) a passionate lithe, dark eyed, olive skinned, firm breasted young lover, spend hours in intense debate about the meaning of life, and suffer sufficiently to give purpose to his dedication. Unsurprisingly his father had not agreed: if the boy had no other more practical ideas of his own for a career, he would use his connections to get him a job; and so he did. After five soul destroying years fiddling monthly readership figures to promote his sales and weekly expenses to supplement his income, Jack left to join the printing corporation of which his father was Chairman.

On joining the corporation Jack had been sent to

various printers within the group all over the country to learn the fundamentals of print from typesetting, to letterpress, lithography and photogravure, and from leaflets, brochures, magazines to books. It was 1963 and a new system of rotary lithographic printing was being introduced; new at the time to Britain although well established for some years in America and Germany. A new system required a new face for its representation it was thought by some obscure rationale, and Jack was to be the new face despatched to a printer in Germany for a month to learn all about it. In the weeks prior to his departure for Cologne he studied German as best he could in the car during lunch breaks; between sandwiches he could listen to the tapes and read the books practising his German accent without the embarrassment of an audience. "Ich bin – du bist".

A joyless day of early spring met Jack on his arrival in Cologne, the cold wet and dreary city made more dismal by chilly gusts of wind from the east coursing down the Rhine valley. The night before, he had kissed his current girlfriend goodbye when they parted, any negative emotions of separation obviated by the anticipated serendipity of his new adventure. On checking in at the Hotel Englebert where he was to reside for his month in town, Jack had been struck equally by the blonde haired towering physique of Herr Englebert the hotel's proprietor on the one hand, and that of his diminutive, dark haired wife to whom he had been introduced on the other. Alone in his room, prostrate on the bed with no desire to explore in the fading early evening light, he visualised the logistics of their sexual coupling, and how such unequally sized persons might communicate when conjoined; should communication become necessary in an emergency, such as in a dire case of asphyxiation. It soon became apparent that Jack was not entirely mistaken in his deliberations, however, for Frau Englebert had found something lacking in her marriage. She was not German but an Irish colleen, and clearly in need of a man with whom she could more easily communicate; not only when vertical, but also when horizontal. Barely a day had passed since his arrival before she made her intentions clear, but Jack was not interested, not out of fear of the physical strength of Herr Englebert – although that was of course a prudent consideration – but out of nothing more than a complete lack of attraction. A French farce ensued: Frau Englebert pursued Jack, and Jack ran.

As a new boy in the printing industry, Jack decided to take a trip over the weekend up the river Rhine to the city of Mainz. He planned his journey as a pilgrimage to the city where Johannes Gutenberg had been born and buried; the first European to invent movable type moulded as individual letters from metal alloys. It was a development that brought about an explosion in the production of books in the 15th century and the subsequent spread of learning: sadly a facility of which Jack had rarely taken advantage.

On the morning of his departure, Jack woke with a raging sore throat and a manly determination to fulfil his intent, stiffened by the need to escape Frau Engelbert and the realisation that there was little else in town to amuse him. Despite his aching throat, Jack sat near the bow of the cruiser as it progressed up river against the current; the previous days of wintery wet had given way to hazy sunshine and a distant promise of spring to come hung in the air. On either side the bleak rows of regimented vineyards blanketed the hills folding down towards the river, with farms and picturesque old villages dotting the countryside. Massive castles and ruined fortresses rose amongst the hills and jagged rocks, historic testaments to the strategic value given to this mighty artery; the *autobahn* of armies and commerce for thousands of years. With the fading light of early evening Jack disembarked at Oberwesel to pass the night in a small inn. Nursing the raging pain of his inflamed throat aggravated by the consumption of a glass of acidic wine at dinner, he fell asleep in his cosy room, the haunting legend of the Lorelei and a siren's song luring ships to their end on the rocks fused with an image of Frau Engelbert tormenting his dreams.

The following morning after an early breakfast Jack re-boarded the cruise ship to continue his pilgrimage arriving at Mainz shortly before midday. It was Sunday. Swiftly disembarking he made his way hurriedly to the Gutenberg Museum only to find on his arrival at 12.05 pm that the museum closed at 12.00 noon for that day and all day Monday. Furious and demoralised, with all desire for further exploration extinguished by the frustration of having made the journey despite his still aching throat, he made his way back to the boat and back to Cologne.

In the evening of his return to the hotel Jack went to the bar; there he knew he would find company, if only the company of strangers with whom he could not converse despite his good intentions. The bar was small and crowded, the whiff of tobacco smoke and stale beer mingling with the unintelligible babble of a foreign language, made more unintelligible for Jack by the fusion of conversation and laughter rising from each group of people seated on the banquette, chairs and tables around the walls. Uncomfortably self aware of the out-of-place conservatism of his English checked tweed sports jacket, cavalry twill trousers and brown brogue shoes which had drawn attention from some at his entrance, he took a tall stool at the bar; Herr Engelbert was barman and spoke a little English so some camaraderie may ensue he thought.

Unlike most young Englishmen genetically wired to the consumption of numerous pints, Jack was not a beer drinker. For him the flavour gave little pleasure, and the volume of liquid in a one pint glass far exceeded the capacity of his bladder to contain it. Alone and ill at ease in this foreign environment, and lacking the inspiration of any immediate alternative, he ordered a beer, casually lighting a cigarette to convey a confidence he did not feel.

"You try zis." Herr Engelbert said with an assuring smile placing a tall straight cylindrical glass of yellowish liquid with a frothy head on the bar in front of Jack. "Kölsch beer very goot."

"Looks good to me" Jack said flippantly raising the glass and drawing off a sufficiently large draught to impress, like a camel draws off water from a pool. "Cologne beer very good" he repeated with a laugh to nourish any seed of fellowship, wiping the froth from his mouth as he replaced the glass on the bar.

With his eagerness to please and the metronomic sipping of his nervous self consciousness, it was not long before Jack had drained the contents of the glass. Even for him, half a pint was feasible. But what Jack did not know was the time honoured tradition of Kölsch: an empty glass uncovered is a request for more and is refilled and refilled until covered. Encouraged by nascent signs of *bonhomie* and the furtive effects of alcohol inciting his resolve, Jack sat and absorbed with fascination the activity in the room around him: the interplay of each table's conversation and laughter in this foreign land, yet so very similar to all he knew at home. Other people's laughter brought a smile to his face, despite having no idea whatsoever as to what they may be laughing about. Flirting on the edges of maudlin sentiment he thought how strange it was that only twenty years before we were killing each other in war, and yet now here he was on a bar stool safe in their land. Oblivious to the realisation that his glass was never empty he continued to consume, all thought of dinner lost in the increasing haze of the present.

"Try zis one, very goot." Herr Engelbert said as he placed a smaller glass of colourless liquid on the bar. "Schnapps."

One schnapps led to another and then another, each glass introduced with the same "very goot" recommendation, and with the consumption of each glass, the snatched and stilted dialogue which had previously passed between Jack and Herr Engelbert became louder, more animated, more confrontational, less considered.

"You strong man?"

Through the turmoil of his increasingly addled mind Jack heard the question and struggled to determine its relevance to anything he may inadvertently have said. But the residue of any thought that may just have been present had already escaped his mind; lost into the convenience of unrecoverable memory. Confused and alcoholically resolute to defend not only his own manliness but also the pride of his nation - the nation that had won the war – and with no concept as to how this light spirited exchange could possibly develop into anything physical, his spirit of bravado rose as his perspicacity declined.

"As strong as you." he heard himself say and regret as the mumbled words dribbled from his lips.

"OK you strong man me strong man. Ve see the strongest." Herr Engelbert pronounced with bright, sober confidence and came around from behind the bar beckoning Jack to follow him.

A murmur went through the room. As their banter at the bar had become more animated an air of animosity had been noted; the primitive instincts of the herd made alert to confrontation. Jack descended from his stool and paused; hours of sitting had numbed his arse and a hint of pins and needles tingled through his legs. Herr Engelbert opened a door at the rear of the room and Jack hesitantly followed down a spiral staircase descending through two floors into an ancient cellar. It was cold and the sweet smell of meat hung in the air from the huge, bloody animal carcasses suspended with hooks on iron rings driven into the ceiling.

Jack looked bewildered, what was expected of him? Were they to wrestle in some no-holds-barred secret, crypto- ritualistic brawl hidden from the eyes of any witness, the winner emerging into the sunlight to claim his right to rule over the clan?

Lying on the damp floor made wet with blood was a quarter of a carcass of wet beef.

"You put meat on hook." Herr Engelbert said indicating the huge bloody mound of flesh on the floor and a ring on the ceiling.

In the semi stupor of his alcoholic state Jack looked at Herr Engelbert and laughed. Surely, he thought, this must be a joke; clearly Engelbert was bigger and stronger. But Engelbert was not laughing; only the smug grin of a bully boy confident of his superior strength showed on his face provoking a determination in Jack not to fail. Oblivious of his clothes Jack bent and grappled with the bloody, wet carcass on the floor, trying to get a firm grip on its floppy bulk. But every time he raised the dead weight from the floor, it slipped and fell back where it had lain. The more he failed the more his determination hardened, and eventually with a supreme effort Jack raised the bloody bulk up, smearing his face as it passed and finally onto the hook. He had succeeded.

In his moment of achievement Jack did not wait to see what Engelbert would do, he was exhausted, soaked in blood from head to foot and in no state or mood to witness what he already knew; hanging the carcasses was an easy task for Engelbert, a job he did every day.

He staggered out of the cellar up the two flights of spiral stairs and, grappling with the handle in the darkness of the stairwell, pushed the door sharply open into the bar. Screams and shouts of fear rose from the crowded room but

Jack did not hear them; at that moment he passed out and fell headlong onto the floor.

When the light of day filtering through curtains finally broke through Jack's unconscious state, he found himself lying clothed on the bed in his room. How he had got there he did not know, and a dull, throbbing ache numbing all cerebral function deterred analysis. Gradually as the stalled functions of his brain cells spasmodically reignited, visual recall of the previous evening's events percolated through into a stark reality: he had been set up. Some provocative actions or wishful words from his wanton wife must have alerted Engelbert unjustly to suspect Jack's intentions, he thought; his pantomime of strength a truly needless warning. Slowly and carefully Jack rose from the bed to remove his stinking, blood soaked clothes which he then left as a pile on the floor to be considered later. Maybe a good dry cleaner could restore the jacket and trousers, he hoped, even if the shirt was beyond recovery. In an effort to cleanse and wash away all the physical and mental residue of the previous night's events, he wallowed unhurriedly in the bath, washed his hair and shaved, slowly retrieving the equilibrium of his senses. When he passed by the front desk in the foyer to leave the hotel for the day with no hint of frailty that may give satisfaction, he offered a bright, smiling "guten Morgen" to Herr Engelbert; a contrived nonchalance dismissive of any importance for what may have transpired.

For the remaining two weeks of Jack's training period in Cologne he avoided the Engelberts as best he could with only the customary "guten Morgen" whenever their paths crossed. When the day came for his final departure he was happy to be going home. He had learned as much as was necessary for his sales task ahead, and was weary of the chilly inhospitality of the city's weather and people. Clearly the purpose of his stay had not been intended as a jolly break from the bleakness of winter at home, but apart from a superficial conviviality that had emerged by day between him and the print workers in their mutual struggle for bilingual understanding, despondency and the menace of latent crime hung in the city's streets after dark.

In London Jack lived in a small apartment in South Kensington in the form of a flat-roofed prefab stuck on the roof of a red brick Victorian building reachable by a lift to the fourth floor, and then by an exterior iron staircase. Shortly after leaving school he had left home to exploit his independence, enduring the comparative squalor of a series of bed sits by week, with the comforts, cooking and laundry of his parental home in the Kentish countryside each weekend. He had been fortunate in finding this singular roof top accommodation through a chance meeting amongst friends in a local pub. The current renter was leaving the country to take up a contract in California for five years, and not wanting to lose the apartment should he then wish to return, he was happy for Jack to look after it for the same monthly rent. The rent was not cheap - beyond the reach of Jack's pocket on his own - so he shared it with Hugh Henderson, a close friend from his days at school.

Although the accommodation was Lilliputian (mini living room with cupboard-kitchen, two mini bedrooms and a bathroom) the ample flat roof surrounding their box was accessible through the bathroom window: an added bonus on summer evenings providing *voyeuristic* opportunities on the intimacies of neighbours. The furniture and furnishings of the flat were dictated by the extreme limitations of its dimensions, but to suggest a greater sense of space and continuity, the walls throughout were painted white, and a mid blue carpet covered the floors of all rooms with complementary patterned curtains. In the diminutive living room were two small wooden Ercol armchairs, a red formica topped dining table for two with stools tucked under, and a flight of bookshelves bolted to one wall. A stylish radio gramophone of walnut veneer on pointed legs - a twenty first birthday present to Jack - dominated the room on which he would listen to Sinatra's "Songs for Swinging Lovers" and other romantic tunes, finding empathy in the emotions conveyed by the lyrics, and relating their sentiments to the turbulent amorous events in his own love life at any particular time.

Despite their different temperaments - or maybe because of those differences - Jack and Hugh had become close friends since they had first met. They were the same age and had started boarding school together in the same term. But while Jack excelled on the sports field and failed dismally in the classroom, the very opposite could be said of Hugh. On leaving school he had gone on to Oxford University; Jack looked for a job. Together they appeared like opposing pieces on a chess board: Jack fair and light-skinned, Hugh dark and swarthy. Jack the salesman was ambitious, impatient, rebellious, and prone to temperament. Hugh the City broker was contained, patient, phlegmatic and loath to cause a scene.

By choice Jack was not a man's man contentedly consuming pints amongst chums. Too easily obsessed by the feminine charms of too many young women he met, he fell in love repeatedly; the all consuming turmoil of each infatuation consuming all until another caught his eye. Through each new period of bewitchment Hugh would be subjected to the agonised emotions of his lovesick friend, the romantic details of "a love unlike any other he had known": the colour of her hair, the soft beauty of her face, her voice, her laugh, her body, her legs, her breasts…..particularly her breasts. Patiently he would listen like a psychologist may listen to the ramblings of a patient on the couch, for that was all that was expected of him, until the sickness passed and the fever subsided.

"You know Hugh the strangest thing is that in the first few weeks after she came to the office, I found her totally frustrating," Jack explained, "not because I was attracted to her, but because she was so inefficient. Her typing was full of mistakes, at times she could not read back her own shorthand, or recall who had phoned when I was out. She's a temp you know, and she told me that when she's earned enough money, she buggers off down to the south coast of Spain - hitch-hikes all the way to a little fishing port place she's found called Torremolinos or something like that – and when her money's running out she comes back to repeat the process. Anyway as time has gone on, gradually I have found myself becoming strangely enticed by her, the irritation of her inefficiency has somehow metamorphosed into an attraction; she's quirky, fun and growing on me. Somehow I can't get her out of my mind. Her name is Biddy - isn't that cute?"

"Jack you can't be doing this" Hugh counselled "It's not advisable to be having a dingdong with a secretary in the office, you know, shitting on your own doorstep etcetera, and anyway, what about Lucy?

"I'm not having a dingdong as you put it."

"Maybe not yet, but you know you want to."

"Why is sex your first and only consideration when it comes to women? Maybe I'm falling in love with her."

"You're already in love with Lucy."

"Well yes, but I'm only telling you about my confusion, the confusion of my growing attraction to Biddy. She's so cute."

"Yes you said she's cute."

"She has long blonde hair held back with a bow and wears these mini skirts with white socks up to her knees, low heeled shoes and cashmere sweaters that hug her tits."

"How do you know she doesn't already have a boy friend, maybe she's also madly in love? Have you asked her?"

"No our conversations have not been particularly personal, but when she talks of hitch-hiking down to the south coast of Spain, she has never mentioned a boyfriend: I've paid careful attention."

"Well maybe before you get totally carried away yet again you should tactfully enquire, you know, just to be on the safe side, you don't want to be humiliated or find yourself embroiled in some punch-up with a jealous boy friend. By the way you haven't answered my question about Lucy. What about Lucy?"

"No of course I'm still crazy about Lucy it's just that this girl's got under my skin."

Jack replied breaking into song. "I've got you under my skin, I've got you…….I'm having supper with Lucy on Friday."

"Well don't pour your heart out to her - I'm not sure it would go down that well."

On the night of Jack's supper with Lucy their conversation was not about love. That morning, another Jack, John F. Kennedy, President of the United States of America had been assassinated, shot in the head as he sat in an open topped car next to his wife Jacqueline in their motorcade through Dallas. Television showed the horror of the scene caught on camera heightening the events, and the murmured news spread through the air like an epidemic infecting all. Such had been the universal optimism personified by the youthful presence of this man, the news of his death was like a massive punch in the abdomen of the western world winding all; a sense of deep despair was the sole expression of every being, and a blanket of depression smothered over all which it passed. The mood in the little local Italian restaurant was uncharacteristically subdued, gone was the theatrical banter of the *cameriere*, and an overt familiarity discreetly conveyed a sense of unity in times of mourning. As they sat in the corner, their natural exuberance dulled, their conversation centred, Jack was relieved, not by the drama of the day's events, but the cynical expediency of the moment: he did not have to pretend, his distracted mood could not betray his thoughts.

"Jack you're miles away." Lucy said softly taking his hand in hers on the table top and gently squeezing to bolster his moral.

"I'm sorry" he said apologetically "this terrible news is such a shock, it's just come out of the blue that's all, hard to take it all in. By the way, are you going down to the country tomorrow?"

"Yes – if you're going down too we could meet up tomorrow evening at The George and Dragon. Tom and Patsy will be there."

"I'm not entirely sure. I seem to remember Hugh mentioning something or other over this weekend. I may stay up in town. If I do come down I'll give you a call."

Jack had determined that the art of selling was the art of disguise and self promotion, the ability to change one's personality to match that of the buyer in the instant of meeting - like a chameleon changes its colour - and the necessity to sell oneself. Confidence in the seller gives confidence in the product being sold. Good looks, humour and smart dressing helped grease the wheels. Despite Jack's conviction in the verity of this analysis and sincere belief in his mastery of these fundamentals, over the few years of his sales experience a flaw had emerged in one aspect of his ability. It was not difficult to match the personality of a client or potential client within the limited time and confines of their offices, but it was extremely testing to feign conversational interest over an extended period when entertaining over lunch in a restaurant. Talk of gardening;

football; cricket; motor bikes; caravans; and camping, for example, tested his ability to sustain a dialogue. A solution must be found, he thought, and he found it in the realms of a totally new experience.

Terry Hall, Jack's sales director, was a man of Wildean wit and a penchant for Prince of Wales patterned suits. Tall, slim, fortyish, with a full head of salt and pepper hair crowning a pitted complexion from adolescent acne, he had taken young Jack under his wing. Jack shared Terry's sense of humour and they had become close colleagues, assisted in part it might be said, by Jack being the son of the corporation's chairman. When Terry first introduced Jack to Jenny's strip club in Soho, it had not been his conscious intention to help solve Jack's conversational problems, but merely as his policy to assist his team in their sales endeavours by whatever means within reason. Through years of experience and close study, he had determined that most men enjoyed watching young women teasingly taking off their clothes, and often reciprocated their appreciation with large print orders.

Jack was soon a regular customer at Jenny's and quickly noted that a convenient by-product of middle aged ogling was that conversation was an unwanted intrusion when concentrated lechery was taking place. Any potential client with whom he knew from experience he would struggle to converse he took there; the way into some men's goodwill lay not through their stomachs. Having previously arranged a suitable table in front of the stage, he ordered drinks and sandwiches, and when the show started and his client was thoroughly engrossed, he slipped off to chat with the girls waiting to go on later.

In time through Jack's regular presence at the club he had got to know Jenny. She was more or less the same age as he and increasingly tactile in conversation, conveying in her manner a desire beyond a client / proprietor relationship. One day as Jack was leaving with Terry, Jenny told him to return alone. She said Bob the doorman would be the last to leave, she would be closing the club for the day, and she wanted Jack to fuck her over the bar. She had the whole scene planned.

Despite his youthful libido, Jack was terrified. All his comings and goings at the club had been nothing more than a convenient commercial expedient: yes Jenny was young and yes she had a ripe, womanly body, but he was not sexually attracted to her. Hastily he tried to explain his dire predicament to Terry who, caught on the hop, advised a retreat to the coffee bar upstairs in the street; a serious discussion must be had.

"My dear chap," Terry advised, "you can't possibly let the young woman down. Clearly she's become attracted to you over time and planned the whole event. I mean just think how many other men would give their eye teeth to be in your position now - not me it must be said - but to shirk your responsibility, well it's just not polite, not gentlemanly."

Jack lit a cigarette to calm his nerves. "I'm sure you're right Terry, but I'm not like those other lecherous old sods that frequent these strip clubs. I'm not at all sexually attracted to Jenny and I'm terrified that if I try to be the gentleman you say I should be, I'll just make a laughing stock of myself and leave her annoyed and insulted anyway."

"OK well if you can't you can't, but at least you should be polite and go back down there and try to explain yourself to her."

"Oh hell, do I have to." Jack found himself saying, like an adolescent instructed to perform an inconvenient task.

"Yes Jack I think you have to, otherwise we won't be welcome in the club again."

Jack reluctantly returned to the club below, everything appeared closed and the staff had gone. At first he thought he was in luck, maybe Jenny had left, it had all been a joke, but Jenny was there awaiting her man, and when Jack fumbled to find the words to explain she was furious, the fury of a woman scorned. Sheepishly Jack left and returned to Terry, but he had gone. Jack never returned to Jenny's, but that was a small price to pay, he thought, at least he hadn't been duped into lifting a quarter of a carcass of wet beef off the floor.

Chapter 2

Recognition Of Love

Jack had met Lucy at a bottle party. They had come across each other previously as children many years before when she had thrown an egg at him. But although their respective parents had known each other socially from a distance for many years, they had never found sufficient mutual interest in each others company for any inter family friendship to develop. When Jack matured into his twenties, therefore, he was unaware of Lucy; that negatively provocative little girl now matured into a tantalisingly provocative young woman. For some months prior to that night's revelry, Jack's lust interest had been vainly concentrated on a willowy blonde named Sarah, but naive enthusiasm denied him the wisdom of subtlety. Like a male bird of paradise frenetically performing plumage displays and dances to impress a mate, so he would do all to attract her attention, while Sarah, genetically programmed to determine the most financially eligible suitor remained coolly detached. Through the haze of cigarette smoke and mingled screen of twisting bodies on the dance floor, Jack caught a fleeting glimpse of a face, a body he did not know – a glimpse of an angel he later recalled to Hugh - and in that moment all thoughts of Sarah evaporated.

Jack circumnavigated the dance floor as nonchalantly as possible so not to betray his interest; the object of his desire was centred in a small group of his friends. "Evenin all," he said in mock cockney, casually opening a packet of cigarettes and offering her one, "I don't think we know each other, I'm Jack."

"Hello Jack. Long time no see. No thank you, I don't smoke." She said smiling.

Caught off guard by her response Jack looked puzzled. "Oh my God how embarrassing, do we know each other?" He said drawing on his cigarette and exhaling.

"About fifteen years ago I threw an egg at you at a kid's party. I'm Lucy Donaldson. Our parents know each other, at least they know **of** each other, but somehow our social paths never cross."

"Now I vaguely remember." Jack said assuming a facial expression of one in serious concentrated thought. "Did you hit me, I mean, with the egg?"

"No unfortunately I missed and it hit the wall, egg all over the place," she giggled, "and it wasn't even our house.

You got all the sympathy and I got hell."

"Well it seems I was lucky you didn't make a lasting impression on me then, but I'm sure if I had known what a truly beautiful young woman would blossom out of that obstreperous little girl, I would have stood firm and taken the full impact of your egg like a man." Jack said with mock gallantry.

"Why sir you're too kind." Lucy responded, and as the compulsive rhythm of Baby Love oh Baby Love blasted off the dance floor, she grabbed his hand pulling him into the mêlée saying "Oh I love this song, let's dance."

Occasionally the music was uninspiring and they broke off: a glass of wine, another beer and chats with friends. Like a dog with a bone Jack kept possessively close to Lucy, indicating in his protectiveness that for the moment "she's with me".

"I can't believe you've always been around and we haven't met." Jack shouted over the pounding music.

"Well I haven't always been around. When I came down from Oxford I went to Paris as an *au pair* for a year to perfect my French. After my contract finished I decided to stay on for another few months; I took a short *Cordon Bleu* course."

"Like Audrey Hepburn in the film Sabrina. What did you take at Oxford?"

"French language and French literature, that's why I

went to Paris to submerse myself in the day to day *actuelité* of the language. It's was a great experience."

"I love Paris. I have an older sister, Emily, living there." Jack said. "She studied at the Sorbonne, met a fellow student, Francois Guichard, and stayed on after they both completed their studies. Later they married and have two kids. In the late summer of 1958 I went to stay with them. At that time Charles de Gaulle was campaigning for a return to the Presidency, it was just after the Algerian crisis. I went to the Place de la République to hear him speak, but I got mixed up in a huge demonstration chanting "*non a de Gaulle, non a de Gaulle*". There were police on all the surrounding rooftops with rifles. The riot police charged at us with batons bludgeoning the people left, right and centre. I ran like hell down all the little side streets to escape" he laughed, "it's a good way to get to know Paris."

"Wow it sounds terrifying," said Lucy suitably impressed, "I heard the police have a pretty bad reputation for their use of force. Does your sister have a job or does she concentrate on being a mum?"

"Her husband works for Hachette the publishers. I think he's an editor, sub editor or something like that. Emily works there too part time, but at the moment the kids are small; a boy of five and a three year old little girl, so they're a bit of a handful."

"I can imagine. Unfortunately I don't have a brother or

sister."

"Your parents put all their chips on one number," Jack laughed, "and that number certainly came up trumps if you ask me."

Lucy smiled at the implied flattery. "Maybe one day I'll ask your sister if she could help me get a job with Hachette, I would love to return to Paris and use my French."

"Wouldn't we all, but my problem is I don't speak French. When I left school I wanted to go to study fine art at Les Beaux Arts. I had this romantic dream of living a bohemian lifestyle in Paris, but it wasn't to be."

"Why not?"

"Well, my father wouldn't collaborate financially, and frankly I suppose I didn't have the dedication. I'm not really cut out to starve in a garret for the sake of my art. Too fond of what I like." Jack laughed. "By the way how do you know Chris our host?"

"I went out with him for a while when we were both up at Oxford together. Nothing too serious though."

"If it's not rude to ask, why did you break up so as to speak?"

"Well we didn't break up as such as we weren't truly together. I think we just drifted apart when I went to Paris."

"He must be mad."

"And you, where did you go, what did you take? I bet you're frighteningly bright and got honours in something fearfully intellectual." Lucy said brightly.

Jack felt the twist of embarrassment, the sting of self conscious discomfort that always accompanied this subject, a feeling of not belonging, being an outsider, a gate crasher, an unqualified member of the club. He lit a cigarette to cover his discomfort.

"That's very generous," he laughed papering over any cracks in his composure, "but I didn't; too impatient to get on, too rebellious for academic study."

"So what do you do if I may ask?"

"I'm in printing, following in father's footsteps."

"You commute to town every day?"

"No I share a small flat in Kensington with Hugh, an old school mate, and come down at the weekends, you know, home cooking, laundry etcetera. Hugh's family come from the west country, somewhere near Bath, so he goes down there most weekends."

"How about you, do you commute from home?"

"No I live with my grandmother in Hampstead during the week and come down most weekends."

"Great, so we can see each other in town, I don't have to wait an eternity until next weekend. Where do you work, somewhere central?"

"Just off Leicester Square. Currently I'm working in a small advertising agency as a secretary. They have a couple of small accounts for companies operating in France so my

French can come in handy sometimes."

From the outset of their meeting that night it was apparent that both Jack and Lucy were more than comfortable in each other's company. Whilst others regularly circulated or formed small coteries of long time buddies drinking and chatting in the secluded darkness of smoke filled corners, they appeared unified in their mutual attraction. Frequently Lucy would grab his hand pulling him onto the dance floor as yet another compulsive rhythm provoked her into tireless action, and as they gyrated unrelentingly to tracts of Motown, The Beatles and others, Jack could not believe his fortune. Was it just the compelling sound and rhythm that was motivating her? He wondered. Was he just an incidental necessity – an obligatory partner in the primitive emotive expressions of dance, or was their meeting their destiny; some mutual force instinctively binding them increasingly together? Looking at her through the stimulated mist of his euphoria with her long blonde hair cascading over her shoulders, dark brown eyes set seductively deep in her beautiful face, a disturbingly attractive figure and vivacious personality, he felt the emotional surge of his attraction for her. He moaned inwardly as if resenting the pain she caused: "She must be the desire of every man in the room." he said to himself. As the night drew on they drew closer; their bouncy Baby Love individuality of only hours before had dissolved, and the emotive strains of Ella's Every Time We

Say Goodbye now bound them tightly together. The light of day was just filtering through the windows, Saturday night had given way to Sunday morning and Jack was painfully in love.

Lucy's parents, Bernard and Joan Donaldson lived in a small, picturesque timbered house dating from the 16th century; the south lodge of a large estate in the heart of The Weald of Kent. The magnificent Elizabethan stately home to which their lodge had once belonged had sadly been burned to the ground at some time in the 19th century and replaced with a red brick Victorian pile. Bernard, tall, slim and balding, with watery eyes in a rosy cheeked face partially hidden behind horned rimmed glasses, was the epitome of his kind in the insurance business. By nature a punctilious bureaucrat, he had joined Universal Insurance as a young man straight from school in the 1920s, and illegible for active service in the war due to his myopia, he had worked his way up to mid management before taking early retirement. In her youth, Joan had been an attractive catch for any man, even working briefly as a photographic model before marriage, an activity then considered somewhat risqué. At the time of their engagement announcement, mute dismay – and a few ribald suggestions - had fluttered through the men folk among their party set, envious that Joan had been snapped up by such a prosaic personality. Now in middle age, time exacerbated by heavy smoking and a partiality for pink gins had taken their toll on her face and figure, exacerbated by casual employment behind the saloon bar of their local pub.

In the afternoon of the day following the party Jack woke reluctantly, crawling out of bed bleary eyed, the fatigue of alcohol consumption and energy expended vindicated by the ebullient memory of Lucy and the night's events. Shaved and bathed he made his way downstairs, mindful of the parental reception he may receive yet again for the hour of his homecoming. From the kitchen he heard the sound of crockery being prepared for tea.

"Good morning mother," he said dutifully giving her a peck on the cheek attempting to allay the anticipated criticism, "or should I say good afternoon."

"Well I suppose we have to be thankful we see you at all."

"I know what you're going to say, and I do appreciate that this is not just a convenient hotel for weekends, but it was a great party and I'm sure you wanted me to have a good time. Come on, you were young once."

"Yes dear, but maybe you could spend a bit more time with us when you do come down, and apart from that, there are so many small jobs that need doing around the house and garden. Your father is totally incapable. The garden is becoming far too much work for poor

Henry to manage on his own now that he's getting

on and I can't find any other gardener that has a clue what they're doing. They don't know the difference between a flower and a weed."

"OK I promise I will spend more time at home next weekend – unless something more attractive turns up." Jack laughed. "Actually, speaking of something more attractive, I met a fabulous girl last night; so beautiful. Her name's Lucy, we spent the whole time together chatting and dancing. She told me you know her parents; the Donaldsons."

"Yes I know who you mean, but we don't know them well, occasionally we've met them at parties, but we don't socialise."

"Why not?" Jack questioned with mildly indignant surprise.

"Well dear your father has very little in common with Bernard Donaldson, and I have very little if anything in common with his wife Joan - she works in a pub."

"Oh Mum, don't be such a snob, if Lucy's mother works in a pub so what?"

"In my day dear only bar maids worked in pubs."

"Well mother times have changed, and anyway, their daughter Lucy is simply gorgeous and I plan to be seeing a lot more of her, if you know what I mean."

"Yes, unfortunately I do know what you mean. Please don't rush into anything and please be responsible, with the exuberance of youth one can get into so much trouble. I remember my father always used to say to me: Be good, but if you can't be good be careful."

"Speaking of trouble, where's Dad?"

"Don't laugh he's out in the garden cutting the dead heads off the roses. He calls it pruning the roses. Anyway it's all a help. Be a dear, tell him tea is ready."

The home of Harold and Phyllis Strange had been a small nunnery at one time, a picturesque composition of timber framed buildings dating from the 17th century set among woodland on a hillside offering panoramic views down to the river Medway and over the Kentish countryside. Surrounding the house were extensive landscaped gardens with lawns, herbaceous borders, shrubberies and a terraced rose garden descending to an ornamental lily pond. Since his youth Harold had been engaged in the printing industry, his father having been the proprietor of a sizeable printing company in Tonbridge before the war, which

Harold had subsequently sold into the corporation of which he had now become chairman. Tall, slim and chisel featured with a well trimmed moustache and a full head of immaculately combed hair, he cut a handsome figure, impeccably dressed, exuding a natural gravitas lending authority to his upright bearing. As a young man in his thirties, Harold had inherited the property from his parents who had expanded the gardens around the house over the many years of their occupation; a time before the war when horticultural labour was easy to find and gardens inexpensive to maintain. Having inherited the property himself it had been Harold's dream that his son in turn would also inherit the house when that time arrived, and in so doing, create a tradition maintaining the property within the family for successive generations. But at that time few had foreseen the degree of social change that would percolate through society in the years following the war, and the penalising top rate of income tax that would prejudice that dream's reality.

Phyllis Strange was the daughter of Sir Archibald Clement, a distinguished High Court judge during the period between the two world wars. Following in her father's footsteps, she had herself qualified as a lawyer before her marriage to Harold Strange, but ceased to practice on becoming pregnant with their first child. After Emily's birth Phyllis did not return to the bar, deciding instead to dedicate herself to her family's welfare and beloved garden; healthy activities enabling her to retain the slim figure and fine boned facial beauty of her youth, assisted by the grace of genetic good fortune. Despite her conservative appearance – cautious cotton frocks in summer, tweeds and twin sets in winter - as the youngest of three sisters renowned in their heyday for their beauty, charm and wit, she had a twinkle in her corn flower blue eyes, and kept alive the spirit of her youth making her popular with Jack's friends; a bridge of understanding in her relationship with her son.

In her customary style Phyllis had set tea on a trolley in the sitting room maintaining the inherent traditions of her upbringing: fine slices of buttered bread composed on a dish lined with a lace doily, with Patum Peperium paste, a variety of jams, a plate of biscuits, and a freshly made Victoria sponge cake which she had baked that morning knowing it was her son's favourite. An ample inglenook fireplace occupied almost one entire side of the room, oak panelling with a gilt mirror and two landscape paintings hung on the opposing wall, and large lead light windows at either end offered views across the gardens to the surrounding fields and woodland. Antique furniture decked with family photos lined the walls, oriental carpets covered the polished wooden floor, and a large cut crystal vase of deep red roses lent a hint of their heady fragrance to the room. It was a perfect English summer day; puffy white clouds floated in a blue sky, the garden a kaleidoscopic confusion of blooms, spiralling midges hung in the air above the pond, and frustrated flies buzzed against the window glass, confused and frustrated by their imprisonment.

Harold entered the sitting room flush faced from his unaccustomed exertions and sank deep into his customary armchair to the left of the inglenook fireplace. "So young man, you decided to return to the land of the living. If you're ever going to manage this property yourself one day, you're going to have to learn to play less by night and work more by day eh? I expect your mother has already given you the - this is not a hotel lecture - so I won't repeat it, but we do expect you to pull your own weight around here from time to time at weekends."

Phyllis looked knowingly at Jack, a look of disapproval dulled by the hint of a smile.

"Yes of course." Jack responded, instinctively aware that immediate appreciation was the simplest manner to placate his father's strictures. "Maybe next weekend I can do something to help Henry, cut the long grass in the orchard? I rather enjoy the savagery of that Alan cutter machine. It's just the gathering up of all the long cut grass afterwards that's rather boring."

"Are you planning to return to London early this evening or staying for dinner?" Phyllis enquired. "As you know your father and I eat lightly on Sunday evenings when your not here, but if you're staying I will have to get something out of the freezer."

"That's sweet of you Mum, but I think I'll crack off after tea if that's OK, make an early start to avoid the traffic."

Despite Jack's relaxed appearance since regaining consciousness he was restless, his mind continuously reverting to thoughts of Lucy. Flashed images of her beauty and effervescent personality on the dance floor the night before dominated his mind's eye, and the intimacy they had shared in the hours before their separation. On previous weekends, having spent the major part of the weekend drinking with his mates or in a state of unconsciousness, he would not have been in any hurry to return to the limited space and comforts of his London pad, but now he wanted to get going as soon as it was politically expedient, as if his getting going would somehow accelerate time and shorten the hours before he could see her again.

"You're back early." The flustered tone of Hugh's mildly accusatory exclamation from the central area of the flat met Jack as he opened the door: a mix of resentment and embarrassment for the surprise of his flat mate's untimely intrusion.

Judging Hugh was not alone, Jack lingered in the passageway allowing his friend time to arrange his situation before he passed hesitantly into the sitting room, uncertain as to what he may find. Hugh adjusted his composure and his friend the buttons of her blouse.

"What brings you back so early?" Hugh asked, endeavouring to obviate any interest in the particulars of his own situation by the confident tone of his rhetorical question. Not waiting for an answer he turned to introduce the young woman at his side. "Oh yes, by the way, this is Belinda," he said self consciously, "Belinda Bateman."

Jack laughed to relieve the accumulated air of discomfort in the room and put out his hand to shake

Belinda's. "Hugh, you old rogue," he said with all the charm at his disposal, "you never let on you were hiding such an attractive creature."

"Don't pay any attention to him," Hugh advised turning to Belinda, "believe me he says that to all the girls, I know I live with him. We met at my cousin's wedding last month. Her parents live near Sherborne, but the really good news is that during the week Belinda lives just around the corner in Bolton Gardens."

Smiling broadly Jack turned to Belinda "So I'm right, you've been hiding Belinda for a whole month," he said with mock seriousness, "keeping her under wraps so that nobody else would have the benefit and pleasure of her company."

"Hello Jack, I'm not so sure I like the creature bit, but I do appreciate the compliment. There has been no hiding going on, Hugh's told me all about you anyway, and I can see already why he advised me to be cautious." Belinda said with a broad smile; a soft, seductive rasp in the timbre of her voice instantly registering on the sensitive gauge of Jack's innate female attraction meter.

"Well we meet now, and Hugh's a very lucky man."

With her short black hair, olive skin, ebony eyes and aquiline nose set on a slender face, Belinda was attractively gamin in her appearance, leaving Jack pondering about those other essential female attributes so important in his judgement. One could easily imagine her being French he ruminated; the exotic thought and evocative voice adding to her appeal.

"Have you eaten?" Jack enquired. "I'm rather hungry and I'm sure there's nothing here. I think I'll go around the corner for a bite; anyone care to join me?"

"Love to but I can't. I told the girls - my flatmates - I'd be back for supper so I'd better get going."

"That's a shame, and just as I was getting to know you." Jack said teasingly. "If they are as tempting as you, I would love to invite all the girls," he laughed, "but I'm only a poor salesman so unfortunately I have to face reality, how about you Hugh?"

"Jack you're incorrigible. OK I'll join you in a minute. I'll just walk Belinda back to her flat and I'll see you at Giovanni's."

Over pizza margaritas and a cheap bottle of wine, Jack poured out the agonising obsession of his new found love for Lucy. In a continuous verbal flow punctuated only by hurriedly masticated forks of pizza and gulps of wine, he related to Hugh in excruciating detail the circumstances of their meeting: the moment he had first set eyes on her, how they had met, the spiralling emotions of his attraction as the night went on, her hair, her eyes, her mouth, the feel and warmth of her body close to his as they danced until dawn.

"Wow," Hugh said when at last he could speak, "and to think that I was getting a little jealous at your peacock display in front of Belinda just now."

"Old habits die hard you know." Jack laughed lighting a cigarette.

"If Lucy's family live so close to yours," Hugh asked, "how come you've only just met this angel?"

Jack explained the story: the egg thrown when they were kids; Lucy's time at Oxford and subsequent *au pair* sojourn in Paris; the clear realisation of his parent's purposeful lack of any social contact whatsoever with her parents; and their inevitable disapproval of his new found love for their daughter Lucy.

"My advice if you want it old chap is don't rush. You've got to admit it you're totally weak when it comes to attractive young women. You fall in love at the drop of a hat, just look at your record. This may prove in time to be the love of your life, but it's not clever to appear too keen. Much better to keep a little distance, play a little hard to get, it will make you more attractive. Remember the lyrics: A man chases a woman until she catches him."

"I'm sure your right Hugh, but I just feel instinctively that Lucy will one day be the one for me. I'm really not too clever at playing hard to get, I'm usually too preoccupied with being easy to lose. Anyway, enough about me, tell me more about Belinda, she's very attractive, how did you get together, and how did you get together behind my back eh?"

"I don't know where you get this ridiculous idea that

I was conducting this clandestine affair behind your back as you put it. I told you, Belinda and I met at my cousin's wedding last month. I found her rather attractive, we got on well, but I only saw her again briefly in London before she went off for two weeks' holiday in Italy with her parents. Last week she phoned me, she wanted to tell me all about their fabulous time in Tuscany. She said she was staying up in town over this weekend, so I did the same; I thought I'd like to get to know her better."

"From your expression and her re-buttoning of her blouse when I came into the room, I would say you were certainly getting to know her better." Jack chortled. "As she phoned you only a few days after her return, clearly she has an eye for you too. What was it you just said: A man chases a woman until she catches him? Have you met her parents?"

"Yes they seem very nice. Her mother is sweet – looks very much like an older version of Belinda – I gather she's rather horse crazy; they have stables and several horses.

I have yet to visit their home which I'm told is a beautiful Georgian house standing amongst landscaped gardens and fifty or so acres of land. Belinda's father is a solicitor."

"He must be rather a successful solicitor by the sound of it, unless it was all inherited."

"So now you know about Belinda when am I going to meet your Lucy?"

"She lives with her grandmother in Hampstead during

the week. We said we'd phone and get together some day this week. Maybe the four of us could meet up for dinner one night? I'll give her a call tomorrow evening and fix up something soon. I can't wait to see her again, the waiting is agony."

"As you're so head over heels in love with this angel, wouldn't you prefer to see her alone?"

"Well yes, in some ways, but I really would like you to meet her, only then will you truly understand the degree of my passion."

At the earliest possible hour the following evening Jack called Lucy at her grandmother's home. All day he had been counting the hours until the time he judged she would reach home from the office, anxious that his call would be too early, allowing him only the option of explaining to a protective granny who it was that was calling her grand daughter, or speechlessly replacing the receiver; the second option being the most likely choice at that critical moment, denying all later should Lucy enquire.

"Hello. Hampstead 1269."

With a flood of relief Jack instantly recognised the cadence of Lucy's voice.

"Lucy it's me, Jack." He said in a conspiratorial tone, imagining the shielding presence of a chaperoning granny close by.

"Jack," she exclaimed excitedly then continuing more

softly, "how are you? It's so good to hear from you. Since we parted I have been so hoping that you would call, and here you are. I'm speaking in a low voice on the phone in the hall. I've only just this minute come in from work."

"Where's granny?"

"Granny is in the sitting room, she's a bit hard of hearing, but I'm still speaking quietly so as not to alert her. I have yet to tell her all about you as you may well imagine. I only came up from the country early this morning and went straight to the office. The train was packed I had to stand all the way."

"After I finally emerged from my bed yesterday just before tea, I told mother my excitement at meeting you. I must say I hadn't intended to do so, but it was a convenient way to block off the criticism I knew would otherwise be coming for my late homecoming. Anyway I was so restless at home yesterday I had to come up last evening, I couldn't get you out of my mind." He said, ignoring Hugh's well intentioned advice.

"Were you trying so hard to get me out of your mind?" Lucy asked teasingly.

"No of course not, but I would rather see you than imagine you; when can we meet?"

"Your offices are in Long Acre and I'm just off Leicester Square so we could easily meet up for a quick lunch tomorrow if you're free."

"If I'm not I'll make myself free. There's a pub I know in Bear Street that serves good food – The Kings Head – how about meeting there at 1.00pm?"

The fine sunny weather of the weekend had given way to the standard conditions of an English summer as Lucy hurried along the rain soaked pavements for her lunch date with Jack, hugging close to the shop front windows to avoid being splashed from large, dirty puddles in the street by mindless drivers comfortably dry in their seclusion, oblivious to any pedestrian discomfort they may cause. Leaving home that morning the day had been warm and dry with no hint of rain so she took no umbrella with her, only a headscarf for protection. Anxious not to be late Jack had arrived early, bagging a small table for two at the far end of the narrow form of the room facing the bar. Realising he may not be easily visible from the entrance door, nervously he kept an eye out for Lucy, periodically bobbing up and down to see over or through the milling lunchtime crowd. In bed in the dark the previous night the thought had crossed his mind that he had never seen Lucy in the day light. Maybe in the subdued glow, moody music and alcohol induced exhilaration of their only meeting, the beauty of that face and body he held so dear in memory, could have been exaggerated and the cruel light of day dampen his enthusiasm. A waft of cool air and the compressed movement of disturbed drinkers reluctantly allowing passage way by the entrance, alerted Jack that another had entered and he stood tall to see that it was Lucy; lecherous stares following the perfume of her pathway. Energetically waving his arms, Jack signalled his position which she acknowledged, pushing through determinedly to her goal.

"You made it." Jack exclaimed with noticeable delight and relief.

"What a bloody awful day." Lucy observed wiping away the rain drops off her nose, removing her raincoat and the drenched fabric of her headscarf releasing the full body of her blonde hair to cascade over her shoulders.

Jack lent forward around the edge of the table taking her two hands in his and giving her a gentle kiss on each cheek, powerfully eliminating in that instant any negative thoughts that may have intruded his mind. Saturday night had not lied. Rain soaked and harried Lucy was truly as attractive by day as she had been by night. "It's so wonderful to see you again," he said self consciously, "the wait has seemed like an eternity."

Chapter 3

Time For Change

By late autumn of the following year, Jack's relationship with Lucy had finally settled, and tempting side attractions soon dismissed. The initial neural overload of being deeply, passionately, obsessively in love which had caused so much pain and anguish, so many tortured moments of emotional insecurity, had calmed into one of a more mature love based on friendship, understanding, caring, the joy of each other's company, and not least, the joy of sex. Fortunately for Jack, Lucy's unspoken resolve to withhold her sexual favours until she was more confident of their relationship did not stand up to the pressures of their mutual desire; facilitated by the recent advent of the contraceptive pill. Jack was not a virgin but he had wanted Lucy to be. In the possessive naivety of his self indulgent immaturity, he shied vehemently from the mental image of another male's organ fervently penetrating the embodiment of his desire; enflamed by the thought of her contented cooperation. In the early months of their relationship, the subject had been the cause of heated conflicts jeopardising their continuation whenever it inveigled its way into conversation, but reason and the fear of losing Lucy came to temper Jack's dogmatism. With the pride of qualification rarely achieved, Jack had lost his virginity with a virgin in London: Lucy lost hers in Paris. Tough though it may be to digest, he learned, what's good for the goose is good for the gander.

Through the first months of Jack's infatuation preoccupations of love outweighed attention to work; a state soon noted by his sales director. At first he had been concerned that Jack was sickening or losing interest in his job, but after calling him into his office for a chat he commiserated, inwardly recalling the distracted emotions of his own youth.

"My dear chap she sounds divine – a child of nature." He remarked after Jack had poured out the ardency of his passion. "You are a lucky young man and I do understand what you're going through, but you must not let it influence your job. Early next year we will have the installation of this large new rotary machine completed. It will require a considerable volume of work to feed it so you must concentrate on your job by day, even if you concentrate on Lucy by night." He laughed mischievously.

Terry Hall's timely encouragement then not only revealed with stark clarity the important place Lucy had come to occupy in Jack's life - banishing illicit thoughts of Biddy and others - but also his determination to prove himself to his colleagues and most of all his father. Each working day he diligently visited potential clients he had researched, producing quotations when requested and entertaining those who showed the greatest viability. But the required leap of faith into an unknown new printing process and its incomplete installation deterred commitment from potential clients. A year later, with the installation of the new press finally complete but little sign of any large contractual work in sight, anxiety pervaded the sales office, and tension the corridor of power. Terry Hall called a meeting with his team.

"How are things going? I see from your monthly progress reports Jack that you're in regular contact with Brian Fisk. I understand he's planning the publication next year of a new magazine. How is that developing, can you tell me any more about it?"

"Yes I have been having irregular meetings with Brian. He's planning to launch a new girlie magazine, you know, like Playboy. I have the impression that it's rather early days though. Occasionally he calls me to clarify aspects of the printing process; time lines, schedules, etcetera. We meet for tea at The Grosvenor House or The RAC."

"Not exactly the locations one would associate with the nature of the publication." Terry chuckled.

"No, particularly when Brian goes through with me some of the highly revealing colour transparencies being considered for the launch issue; stimulating to say the least I must say, but if others could see what we're studying minutely through the magnifying glass to avoid possible litigation, they'd spill their tea in shock. Anyway, he's getting together a complete dummy so that we can have a firm basis on which we can quote, based on twelve issues a year."

"Try to push that if you can, the sooner we quote the sooner we enter negotiations and, hopefully, secure our first large contract."

"While on the subject of girlie magazines, I also had a short but interesting meeting with Bob Guccione at his home in the Kings Road the other day. I really didn't expect to get an interview with him in person, and certainly not at his private home, but I must say he was very amiable, disconcertingly quietly spoken, not at all the appearance of the man one would imagine as being the founder of Penthouse magazine. His home was beautifully furnished, very modern with stunning abstract art. Anyway, it was an interesting experience but proved to be only polite conversation, at least for the time being, as he had already placed the print contract for the first year's production."

It was not to be until the spring of the following year that all Jack's determined efforts finally paid off, and he received the confirmation order for the first year's print production of Mayfair magazine; he was thrilled. A buzz went through the sales offices. Months of diligent work had come to fruition; it was to be the first large contract, a start in feeding the hungry new rotary press which had been standing idle since the completion of its installation. When the managing director called Jack down to go to his office he was relaxed, convinced that he was to be congratulated; maybe even a welcome salary rise crossed his mind.

"Good morning Strange thank you for coming down."

Douglas Follet, the managing director, exuded all the disciplined qualities of the ex army man that he was, the youngest Major in the force in his day it was said. Short in stature, Napoleonic in character and bone dry in personality, he had come into the printing industry in a management capacity at the age of forty plus, gaining a reputation for ruthless efficiency, and quickly rising to company board level.

"I understand from Mr. Hall that we've received the print contract for Mayfair magazine."

"Yes, as you may know it has been a long time coming, but at last we have a significant contract to feed the new press. It's a beginning." Jack answered with modesty.

"Well I have just informed Mr. Hall, and I must now also inform you, that we will not be accepting this contract."

"What?" Jack exclaimed with indignant disbelief. "The new press has been standing idle for months costing I don't know how many thousands per day without an ounce of income, and the company has decided to turn down this contract? It's just not feasible. The value of this contract may not entirely cover the costs of the machine time it occupies, but at least it's a substantial contribution and will give the machine minders valuable practical operating experience. By covering the major part of its costs, other work we secure in time will have a greater chance of contributing towards a profit. Turning this down is madness; it has taken me months of negotiation. With respect I don't think you appreciate how hard it is to secure orders of this magnitude, your print experience has always been in management. You have little knowledge or experience of sales and the highly competitive market in which we have to operate. We have had to fight against every other large printer in the country capable of handling a monthly magazine production. If you turn down this contract there will be a queue of our competitors fighting to grab the job."

"Don't be impertinent Strange, I didn't ask you to see me in order to debate the subject merely to inform you of the board's decision. It has been decided not to accept the order as we do not wish our company name to be associated with this pornographic trash. You don't have to have experience in sales to secure this work. Anyone can find jobs of this nature if they look in the dustbins of London. Mr. Hall will be notifying the publisher immediately." He said dismissively.

Jack was quiet, quickly thinking through his next move. "The problem as I see it Mr. Follet is that you are out of touch, divorced from the changes that are now taking place in society across the board in this country. The bigotry of the old order is fading fast, social attitudes are changing and the accent is increasingly on the purchasing power of youth. The young are rapidly gaining more importance in the market, taking over with fresh ideas. Frankly I do not wish to be stuck working in a company that is itself stuck in the past century, so I will be resigning my job, but before doing so, it is only correct that I explain my reasons clearly in person to my father."

Turning and leaving the office abruptly, Jack crossed the corridor to his father's office directly opposite, knocking and entering without pause, aware that Mr. Follet was following close on his heels. Seated behind his large mahogany desk Harold Strange looked up, instinctively aware that some tense atmosphere had bull dosed into his space.

"I apologise for entering your office directly without notice, but I have just been informed by Mr. Follet that the order for Mayfair magazine - for which I have been working on hard for the best part of a year - has been rejected by the board. Frankly I find the decision beyond belief in the competition of today's market, but I'm sure you know all about it. I have just given my verbal resignation to Mr.

Follet, but before confirming it in writing I have to know: with all your years of sales experience, do you agree with Mr. Follet or is this decision reversible?"

Harold Strange remained seated, sphinx like in his composure. By nature he did his best to avoid conflict, inwardly knowing his son was right, but unable by his position to take the young man's side. "Jack that's an unfair question and you know it. Regretful though it most certainly is, sadly in the circumstances I have no option other than to accept your resignation. Please confirm it in writing to your sales director Terry Hall."

Having made his decision in the heat of the moment Jack was depressed when he met Lucy that evening; uncertain of the wisdom of his actions and what and where his future may now lie. In the hours since resigning there were moments when he drew comfort from the recognition that he had always been rebellious by nature with a history of kicking over the traces, but somehow matters had generally worked out well. His past was a record of flying off the handle and apologetic redemption, but this time, in the cold light of quiet reflection, the issue appeared more significant: his future career, economic security, and thereby the feasibility of his own aspirations with Lucy.

"I have an uneasy suspicion I may really have fucked up this time, if you'll excuse my French." He laughed uneasily.

"Fortunately, being fluent in French, I understand

completely." Lucy responded to lighten the mood. "Of course you were angry with the stupidity of their decision after the months of work you put in to get the order. Actually when one thinks rationally about it, they have known for months that you were after this deal, so why could they not have made their parochial decision months ago, and saved you all a lot of wasted time. Anyhow what is done is done, don't dwell on it, you certainly don't want to change your mind, and frankly I'm rather pleased that you're not going to be involved any more, ogling at all those naked girl's tits on a month by month basis. If you're going to ogle anyone's tits they had better be mine." She giggled. "I tell you what, now you're on a sort of enforced holiday period, why don't we take advantage and plan a short trip: we could go to Paris to see your sister?"

"It's a great idea and you're absolutely right," Jack said noticeably pulling

himself out of his reflective despondency, "it's really a waste of energy to dwell any more on those silly buggers, but what I must do if possible before we think of going off anywhere, is to think carefully what it is I really want to do in future and get a job; something definite to come back to. I'll start first thing tomorrow."

Earlier than usual the next morning Jack was actively engaged in what he had determined would be his goals for the day. His night's sleep had been shallow, made restless by a tangled thicket of mental imagery, and with each new thought and plan drops of adrenalin radiated his system making him toss and turn. He had not seen Hugh the previous evening to divulge the news, and the frenzied morning imperative to shave, grab a piece of toast, tea and rush, subjugated all other issues until next convenient. Although officially he had to complete the month's notice of his contract, he decided to remain home undisturbed; his loyalty to company of yesterday guiltlessly transposed to himself. Since joining his father in the printing industry, he realised that he had never taken time to reflect on the degree of satisfaction he derived from the daily routine of his working week. It was a job not a dedication, and like most others, it was a means to an end. Now, at the age of twenty six, churning over in his mind the reality of his situation and ambitions with clinical analysis, all became clear: above all else he was by nature creative and needed to find a suitable position in a creative company.

One of Jack's potential clients and a man with whom he could amiably relate and communicate over lunch without recourse to Jenny's strip club was Bill Harris, boss of his own small graphic design studio with offices just off Bond Street. Bill was a talented free spirit, a man in his mid thirties, dismissive of the imposed conservatism of irresolute management who had left the creative department of the advertising agency where he had previously been employed to set up on his own,. Jack called him to have a chat.

"Good morning Bill, don't worry I'm not chasing you for work, at least not in the sense of any previous appointments I have sought with you."

"Hello Jack. Sounds ominous, what's up?"

"It's a little difficult to spill all on the phone, is there any chance I could pop in and see you some time today?"

t"Hold on I'd better check my diary – I don't really keep a diary but it sounds impressive anyway." He laughed and there was a pause. "OK when were you thinking of coming by?"

"How are you fixed for late morning, say twelve thirtyish?"

"It sounds to me as if you're after a favour - you haven't knocked up some bird have you?" He chortled, "Come around at one and you can take me out for lunch."

Over beer and sandwiches in a local pub, Jack spilled out the details of the previous day's events culminating with his resignation; endeavouring to discern from the response of Bill's facial expressions as he spoke, the degree of his agreement and commiseration for the impulsive decision he had made. Over the years of their commercial relationship Jack had felt comfortably at ease in Bill's company sensing a mutual empathy, and whilst no business had transpired between them during that time, Bill had enjoyed Jack's revelations of his production meetings with Mayfair magazine, and erotic photographic details, particularly those rejected as being too explicit.

"That's a bloody shame." Bill proclaimed. "I was looking forward to my monthly free copy from you. I suppose this means I'm going to have to spend money."

"I know Bill I know," Jack said in a tone of feigned commiseration, "That's why I wanted to break the news to you personally so that you'd have time to come to terms with the situation." Jack responded not certain of Bill's real sentiments.

"Well what are you going to do now Jack, do you have any plans, or is it all a bit too fresh? I mean this only happened yesterday you say."

"To be blunt Bill I need a job." Jack replied. "I do not want to drift, take time out to go on an extended holiday, and I really do not want to continue in printing, at least not directly. By nature I'm creative and I would love to be involved in the creative side of the graphics industry. I'm not trained as a designer as you know, but I'm trained in print, a good salesman and," he paused to gather strength for the jump, "I could be a bloody good salesman for you – help you to expand; grow your business."

Bill did not respond immediately, contemplating the proposal Jack had just made. "You know Jack," he then said, "I've never stopped to consider a possibility such as the one you're proposing, so you've caught me a little on the hop.

Since I set up my own studio I must say business has always come to me. I've been lucky perhaps, but it's not getting any easier, and I'm getting too busy with all the different aspects of each production also to take care of looking for new clients and growing the business as you say. Maybe I would benefit by having some lay about such as you peddling my wares." He laughed. "You see I was right, I knew you wanted a favour, it's just that I didn't think it would be this big. Jack I can't tell you now of course, but you've put an idea into my head, I'll get back to you, I promise."

With each new day over the following week Jack woke with a sick feeling of unfulfilled expectancy. Seven days had passed and Bill had not called. At times his spirits were high confident of a positive decision in his favour, others of gloom and negative anticipation. For some time he did not see Hugh at the flat for long enough to tell him the full story, but finally when he had the opportunity, his response was one of loyal support with an undercurrent of incredulity.

"Jack I'm truly sorry that you find yourself in this situation. I really do understand that you were upset by loosing the contract after having put in so many months of hard work, but don't you think you may have rather over reacted? It's a set back, sure, but is the issue of sufficient importance for you to have decided to sacrifice a promising career on the altar of a bum and tit magazine?"

"For God's sake Hugh don't you understand? It's not the

bloody magazine I give a shit about, it's the fact that I was employed to find work for a machine that's been standing idle for months, and the sheer stupidity that having secured an order that will allow that machine finally to operate, they reject the contract because of their bloody, bigoted, parochial conservatism. They knew I was working on this potential project. Could they not have told me from the outset not to waste my time?"

Since his meeting with Bill Harris, Jack had not attempted to pursue any other possible contact. Until he heard either way from Bill he had decided to keep all his eggs in that one basket. In the parks the mellow optimism of autumn's glory had finally succumbed to the cold easterly gusts of winter, and each day seemed an eternity; empty of diversions that could occupy his mind with sufficient intensity to submerge the tension of waiting for an answer. And then the call came.

"Hello Jack it's me, Bill." The voice announced in a restrained tone.

After the days of his anxious waiting Jack was strangely ill prepared, the uncharacteristically impassive tone of Bill's voice shooting a bolt of negativity through his guts.

"Oh hello Bill how are things going?" He said with as much nonchalance as he could muster, as if caught by the unexpectedness of the call.

"Have I caught you at a bad time....in bed?" He

continued laughing much to Jack's relief. "I promised to call and I apologise that it has been so long in coming, but we're very busy and I needed to think long and hard about your proposal."

All Jack really wanted was a simple yes or no, but instinctively he knew he must be patient, a decision would surely have been made, but any indication of over eagerness could negatively influence any contract negotiations were the answer to be positive.

"Look Jack I don't want to….."

"That's OK Bill I quite understand." Jack interrupted anticipating the completion of the sentence.

"Listen you silly bugger let me finish. I wasn't going to say anything decisive. I really need you to come by the office. I think your proposal has some merit, but I need to chat it over with you, see what you're looking for, and if we can find a way forward for our mutual benefit."

"I'm sorry Bill. That sounds encouraging. Whenever is good for you, I'll fit in?" Jack replied with relief, aware that any stay of execution kept open the door of opportunity.

"You can buy me lunch again. Teach you not to interrupt." Bill laughed. "Let's say tomorrow at one. Come to my office and we'll take it from there."

One o'clock took a long time in coming the following morning. Jack was impatient to get going yet apprehensive of the outcome, confident on one hand they could reach an agreement, but conversely that his hand was weak. He had sought a great favour and Bill held all the cards. What was his best game plan? He repeatedly asked himself. He knew from experience that the art of selling a product lies first in the ability to sell oneself in order to gain the client's confidence, and then on the back of having achieved that goal, to sell the product. But in this case he was the product.

When Jack walked out of the pub at 3.00 pm all was resolved and he was elated, the tension of those anxious days and sleepless nights of waiting now made futile by the candid simplicity of their conversation. He had the job he wanted on terms to make it an exciting challenge, and was impatient to get started. Having expressed his gratitude and said his goodbyes to Bill as they parted, a rush of relief from the past days' tension coursed through his mind, and in the light-headed buoyancy of the moment he made a decision: he could now marry Lucy if she would accept his proposal.

"Well how did it go?" Lucy asked animatedly when they met that evening.

"Well"......Jack paused attempting a depressed tone and facial expression to convey disappointment but could not sustain his excitement. "I got the job," he exclaimed jubilantly, "and I start officially immediately after the New Year, although I will be going into their offices during December, just to get myself acquainted."

Lucy rose and leaned over from the banquette wrapping

her arms around him. "I'm so thrilled for you. You're a man of action Jack Strange," she said with pride, "you see if you hadn't taken the initiative and gone to Bill Harris with your proposal, you'd still be looking in the situations vacant columns for a job."

"Darling".......Caught in the thrust of his enthusiasm to pour out his good news, Jack was tempted to spill out his decision to ask her to marry him, but stopped dead in his tracks; this was not the place or time, and another romantic notion had entered his mind. "Now that I can relax in the knowledge that I do at least have a job, maybe we could escape to Paris as you suggested, just for a long weekend, introduce you to my sister I know she's keen to meet you."

"That's a great idea, a weekend in Paris to celebrate. I'm dying to meet Emily. We can do some Christmas shopping."

Jack thought hurriedly to protect the intricacies of his plan. "If you agree I would rather we didn't stay with Emily. I know she would love to have us, but the kids are a real handful at times, and I'd prefer to be independent if you don't object. If anyone asks we'll say we're staying with Emily – I'm sure she'll collaborate – but let's stay in a hotel. We will of course see her."

"Jack Strange that's an immoral suggestion, I'm really surprised by you." Lucy giggled with a twinkle in her eye.

Despite its anglophile spelling, The Family Hotel on Rue Cambon in Paris was consummately French; small and stylishly art nouveau in its flamboyant décor; the serpentine staircase rising from the hall around a lift in the form of a large bird cage, elevated by a hydraulic piston mechanism allowing passenger ascent but no descent. Jack had recalled the name of the hotel from a client's racy tales of illicit weekends: central, cheap and ideally located directly opposite the rear entrance to The Ritz. Their room was small, white and simply decorated, made cosy by the hazy winter sunshine filtering in through the window offering evocative views over the neighbouring roofs.

"Monsieur et Madame Strange." Lucy said with contrived sophistication. "I rather like the sound of that. Just as well they only asked for your passport."

Jack wrapped his arms around her giving her a kiss, noting the comment but avoiding the temptation to react. "The French are rather more pragmatic in this way, if they were not I suppose small hotels like this would lose most of their business." He laughed. "Well this is your Paris and the weather's fair so show me your city. I told Emily we would come by this evening.....she's invited us for dinner."

"You already know Paris."

"Yes I know Paris, but only to a degree as I told you, running away from the riot police, but you spent over a year here so you know places I have not seen."

"Do you know the central market area of Les Halles?"

"No. I heard about it but never went. I must say at that

time in my life the allure of a vegetable market didn't excite me that much. Being mixed up in a riot seemed just a touch more exciting somehow."

"It's not just a vegetable market as you may imagine. It's huge, a wonderful, bustling fresh food market offering everything imaginable, full of colourful French character with divine brasseries where one can eat absolutely delicious food." Lucy said enthusiastically. "We could make our way there on the metro, look around and have lunch."

"It sounds good to me. Over lunch and a glass of wine or two we can make a plan, I know you want to go shopping."

"Did you ever go to the catacombs or take a boat ride in the sewers?"

Jack laughed in disbelief. "Buried bones and floating excrement. Huh, now there are a couple of good ideas for tourist attractions."

"No really, we should do it it's fascinating, something different from the usual sites. The catacombs are ancient stone mining tunnels a few kilometres long with the sides of the tunnels thickly lined high with the bones and sculls of as many as six million bodies relocated from many old church cemeteries in the 18th century. It's a little spooky, so one shouldn't lose the group and get lost." She chuckled. "I think the entrance to the sewers descends somewhere near the Quai d'Orsay. From memory it's not at all claustrophobic, the departure point for the boat ride is ample with a high vaulted ceiling, and the boat goes along the wide sewer canals with a guide explaining the location in the city directly above. One sees no poo or anything nasty, and there are really no smells; it's interesting in an adventurous, peek-behind-the scenes sort of way."

"OK darling, but let's talk over lunch, although on second thoughts talk of sewers may not be a suitable subject for any meal time."

Although keen to be revisiting his favourite city and grateful for the blessing of an unusually warm spell of early winter weather to help sustain that belief, inwardly Jack was obsessed with only one issue: his marriage proposal to Lucy. In his mind's eye he had imagined the unutterable romance of the occasion, but now in the location of his choice, he must perfect the event with the right time, place and circumstance. Through the introduction of a colleague with dubious contacts in Hatton Garden, he had arranged an engagement ring to be made in the form of a diamond and sapphire coronet cluster with payment in cash to avoid purchase tax. He carried the little box in his jacket pocket at all times to avoid loss or premature discovery, nervously checking periodically to insure its existence whenever the devil of doubt entered his mind.

Emily and her family lived in a compact, three bedroom apartment on the second floor of a 19th century building in a quiet street just off the Avenue de Clichy, with the convenience of two metro stations nearby. As Jack and Lucy climbed the stairs to his sister's apartment that evening, the aroma of resident scents trapped in the confines of the stairwell sparked distant memories. Could it really be that five years or more had passed since last he had stayed with his sister in Paris, he asked himself, before the arrival of the children? Smiling inwardly he recalled the reassuring misinformation given to Lucy's parents of their staying with his sister Emily, and his feeble excuses to Emily for staying in a hotel. Of course he knew the two kids could have shared a room together for the few days of their visit, but the thought of the risk of their excited intrusion into the bedroom at an inconvenient moment in the early morning would be embarrassing.

"She's so sweet and attractive." Emily had whispered into his ear as they walked from the front door through into the sitting room behind Francois and Lucy; the two little kids excitedly running ahead dressed in their pyjamas. "And I can already see from his close attention and dopy expression that Francois is suitably dazzled. She also speaks good French which is bound to impress."

"I need to have an opportunity of a quiet word with you at some time." Jack said conspiratorially. "Don't look so concerned, nothing wrong or underhand."

"Jules, Isabelle, have you said a proper hello to Uncle Jack and his friend Lucy?" Emily asked the children in

English as they jumped in excitement on the sofa, and then turning to Jack. "They were so excited you were coming, I had to let them stay up to see you, but have a drink with Francois now while I settle them down or they'll never go to sleep. I'll join you in a minute."

"You speak with them in English Emily?" Lucy remarked.

"Yes it's so important they learn to speak good English, they're already bi-lingual. I always speak with them in English and Francois speaks with them in French."

After dinner Jack strategically got up to help clear away the dishes creating a situation in which he could be alone in the kitchen with Emily leaving Lucy to be entertained by Francois.

"Well let me take these dishes out to the kitchen." He said purposefully standing.

"No Jack please leave it I'll clear it all tomorrow; I'm not working."

Jack looked at his sister facially indicating his need to talk privately. "I insist it will not take a minute and then we can all relax. It's a great opportunity for you Lucy to polish up your French with Francois."

In the kitchen Jack hurriedly explained to his sister his secret marriage proposal plan; he had the determination, he had the ring, but he needed a suitably romantic venue. What could she recommend? No word of his intentions had been said to their parents or Lucy's parents, and he had not gone through the formality of asking her father for her hand in marriage just in case she said no.

"Oh Jack how terribly exciting. I'm so happy for you both. Not much chance of her saying no, one can see from the way she looks at you she's very much in love."

"Well what do you think? I have in mind a small cosy, *haute cuisine* restaurant, nothing too touristic. Dinner would be preferable so we can drink in celebration and soon fall into bed." He laughed.

"I know just the place: Chez Bouchard up in Montmartre. It's in a little street close to Le Moulin de la Galette. It's one of our favourite spots, cosy and not too expensive."

"Wonderful. I trust your judgement. Is there any chance you could make a reservation for us for tomorrow night, say 8.30 pm? I'll phone you late tomorrow morning to confirm if it's OK."

"What were you two gossiping about?" Lucy enquired as they returned to the room.

"Oh nothing, just brother and sister family talk; how's her French Francois, pretty good no?"

"*Très bien*......most unusual for an English person." He laughed.

The following day Jack and Lucy did not go to the catacombs or descend into the sewers; they went shopping.

The realisation that they were only in Paris for a long weekend and that the next day was Sunday with all the shops closed, speedily convinced Lucy to review her day's suggestions. Although nervous at the life changing significance of his decision for that evening, Jack remained purposefully impassive as they dressed to go out for dinner, making light of the reservation, but hailing a taxi in the street for the comparatively inconvenient location of their destination.

"I suppose you know Montmartre well?" He asked making conversation in the taxi as they climbed up the hill towards the Sacré-Coeur starkly illuminated in the darkness.

"Not so much. I came a few times during my time in Paris as it's so associated with the Belle Époque and all the famous artists and their studios at that time. It's well worth coming up at night, the view out over the glittering lights of the city below is spectacular."

There were few people about in the area as the taxi wound its way through the cobbled streets, the warmth of the day's wintery sun lost into the clear starlit sky. In the square a clutch of optimistic artists still sat beside their canvases wrapped against the cold night air, ever hopeful to exploit the romance induced euphoria of any passing tourists. The taxi stopped beside a little restaurant.

"Voilá. Chez Bouchard." The driver announced

cheerfully as if producing a rabbit from a hat.

Three vacant tables with red gingham table cloths and chairs sat despondently on the pavement in front of the red painted façade with Chez Bouchard elegantly centred in white script, and a welcoming warm glow shone out through the windows from its interior. Jack paid the taxi and they hastened inside expectant of the bustle of busy waiters, animated conversation and laughter, but there was none; the restaurant was empty of clientele. Two waiters dressed in white shirts with long black aprons wrapped around them from waist to heels stood smiling invitingly, and a maître d' hôtel dressed impeccably in black tie and tails came forward to greet them.

"Bon soir monsieur, bon soir madame." He said graciously.

"Bon soir." Jack and Lucy responded in unison.

"Just as well we booked." Jack murmured.

"Vous avez une reservation?" The maître d' enquired.

Jack was tempted by a facetious response but thought better of it doubting a Gallic appreciation of British irony.

"Bien sûr," Lucy quickly assured, sensing Jack's rising temperament, "Monsieur Strange."

The maître d' studied a book on a podium which appeared to have little content other than one line. "A oui Monsieur Strange." He said noting the one line and looking up smiling in encouragement leading them to their table.

The interior was compact, cosily intimate and pristine in its nightly presentation.

Crisp white tablecloths, erectly formed napkins, gleaming glasses and cutlery awaited on tables with banquette seating lining the walls on either side. A small grouping of other tables occupied the limited area between. Wood panelled walls in floral art nouveau style framed paintings of imaginary Parisian burlesque scenes from the Belle Époque period, illuminated by the warm glow of suitably styled brass sconces.

"I thought the French ate early." Jack commented, "If no others turn up, we'll be a bit lonely I'm afraid, do you mind?"

"No, not really," Lucy responded, "of course it always adds to the atmosphere if there is more going on, but maybe this is more intimate......exclusive private dining." She chuckled.

The maître d' brought the menus and wine list which Jack appeared to study with the air of a connoisseur, reluctant to lose face by betraying his ignorance. The À La Carte menu was in French, but there he had Lucy to translate.

"Do you like snails?" She enquired looking up from the menu.

"No." Jack responded emphatically. "I tried them once on a return trip before catching the ferry in Calais. I was so hideously ill that I've never tried again since. Maybe it was the sea crossing, but just the thought of snails is enough for me."

Having agreed on the advisability for them both to include garlic, they settled on *Moules Bourguignon* as a *hors d'oeuvre* followed by *Fillet de Boeuf Maître d'Hotel* for her and *Fillet de Boeuf Café de Paris* for him together with a bottle of Saint Émilion, Merlot. Throughout the dinner, oblivious to being alone with only the waiters for company, solely the occasional oohs and aahs of their culinary appreciation of the deliciousness of the cuisine, punctuated the chatter of their incessant conversation. But Jack was inwardly anxious; the small box in his pocket reminded him of the reason for their being there, he must choose the appropriate moment.

"Darling there's something rather important I must ask you." He said putting his hand across the table concealing the box under his palm.

Instinctively Lucy put her arm out to take his hand across the table, but he didn't turn his hand. "Jack you look so serious, what's up?"

Summoning up all his courage in the knowledge that once said it would be seriously embarrassing to change his mind he asked. "Darling will you marry me?"

In that moment of asking Jack turned his hand to reveal the little box, his face red with the self conscience theatrical staging of the proposal, and maybe the wine. Lucy looked down at the little box on the table, her face aglow with surprised delight as Jack opened the box to reveal the ring.

"Yes, yes, yes," she blurted out and immediately burst into tears. "I'm so sorry, it's silly of me I know, it's come as rather a shock, but I'm so happy Jack, what a truly beautiful ring."

"Darling I wouldn't have asked you if I had known it would make you cry." Jack offered jokingly. "The waiters will think I've seriously insulted you or something. Here, give me your hand."

As Jack gently put the ring on Lucy's finger he was unaware that the waiters already knew of his intent; Emily had informed them when making the reservation. Throughout the evening they had patiently been waiting for this moment; a bottle of champagne ordered by Emily and Francois concealed on ice to celebrate the significance of the event.

"Many congratulations monsieur et madame." The maître d' said in English as he proudly brought the bottle of champagne on ice to the table, opening it with a professional flourish; the theatrically induced explosion sending the cork flying across the room. "Voila, a gift to you from Monsieur et Madame Guichard." As he poured two glasses and stood aside, the waiters reappeared together with five others from the kitchens. One opened two bottles of red wine pouring eight glasses and they all stood with glass in hand smiling broadly. The maître d' raised his glass and made a toast. "A votre santé, bonheure et longévité," to which a waiter brightly added, "et beaucoup des enfants." sending all into diffident laughter.

Jack and Lucy stood to receive the toast and then came to shake hands with each of the staff thanking them profusely for their hospitality and kindness. To the maître Jack said "You and your staff have given us a wonderful memory for our lifetime. We will never forget the joy of this evening. Thank you." With tears of happiness in her eyes

Lucy gave him a light kiss on each cheek "Merci mille fois." was all the lump of emotion in her throat would allow.

Sitting back at the table, reluctant to leave the warmth of human spirit in which they had so unexpectedly been wrapped by these kind strangers, Jack and Lucy sipped champagne until instinct indicated the time had come to settle the bill and say their goodbyes.

"You see," Jack commented rising from the table, "one never knows what's in store. We thought it would have been nicer to have other diners keeping us company, but who could have predicted the rewards of such a glorious evening."

Out on the street they turned to wave but the door had been closed. Only the vacant tables and chairs on the pavement, the red façade with Chez Bouchard in white script lettering, and the warm inner glow remained to recall the naivety of their arrival; as if all that had transpired within had been a dream instantly evaporating into the night air.

"Are you cold?" Jack asked.

"No I've got my love to keep me warm." Lucy giggled.

"Then let's walk a bit, breath some fresh air."

They walked down all the steps from the Sacré-Coeur and caught a taxi at the bottom back to the hotel. The night porter was dosing at the desk as they crept by silently taking the stairs to their room.

Chapter 4

Beach Revelations

On their return from Paris, with the enthusiastic acceptance of his marriage proposal and his new job supporting his confidence, Jack and Lucy drove down to the country on the Friday evening of the following weekend to proclaim the good news to their parents. Finding her mother in the kitchen, Lucy ushered her through into the sitting room where her father was engrossed in the newspaper, whispering confidentially that they had exciting news to share.

"Jack has asked me to marry him and I very happily agreed." Lucy announced excitedly.

A look of contained delight passed between the two parents.

"I'm feeling mildly guilty that I did not ask you formally for your daughter's hand in marriage before my proposal." Jack quickly said to Bernard. "But to be frank, I was not entirely sure she would accept me, so I didn't want to alarm you unnecessarily." He chuckled.

"It's good of you to comply with convention now Jack," Bernard responded with a twinkle in his eye, "but you've done it, and Lucy has enthusiastically agreed apparently, so I suppose we're stuck with it."

"Daddy!" Lucy exclaimed in horror.

"I'm afraid it looks that way." Jack responded, reading correctly his future father in law's light hearted need for mock admonishment.

"I will never be so happy to be stuck with anything as I will be to be stuck with you in our family." Joan chuckled wheezily stubbing out her cigarette, "Now we need a drink to celebrate."

Bernard came over to Jack with a grin on his face and shook his hand firmly. "Congratulations, you're a lucky man and I'm confident you will prove to be my favourite son in law."

"Daddy you've only got one daughter."

"Yes I know that's why I am confident of my prophecy." He laughed.

Joan hugged her daughter. "I'm so happy for youdarling, and I must say you're a lucky girl too." She said turning to give Jack a kiss. "Have you thought of a date for your wedding? Don't leave it too long; extended engagements are not a good idea in my opinion."

"It's very early days and we haven't settled on any date

yet, but we're thinking of next May sometime." Lucy offered. "May is a beautiful month – if the weather is good – and the gardens look glorious."

When Jack warily informed his parents that he was to marry Lucy, the news came as no surprise. While there had been no social contact between them and her parents in previous years, during the many months of Jack's single minded courtship, when every indication was that this moment would inevitably arise, they had invited Bernard and Joan to cocktails or dinner several times. Initially this tactic had been done strategically in order to negate Jack's accusations of snobbery, but over time they had discovered a kind and amusing conviviality in Bernard, although Phyllis was still uneasy in her social embrace of Joan.

Jack and Lucy were married on Saturday 15th of May in Saint Mary the Virgin parish church of Chiddingstone. In subtle recognition of her father's limited resources, Lucy had firmly assured that the event was a modest affair with guests limited to family and close friends. Ivy Stoaks who had remained affectionately attentive since first teaching Lucy as a little girl in the village primary school also attended, together with Jack's nanny, Doreen Wilkes, and Henry Reader the gardener: staff past and present who had witnessed his development from boisterously self willed little boy to this proud moment of mature commitment. The interior of the ancient church was gloriously decorated in a heavenly scented profusion of flowers professionally arranged by a friend of Lucy's mother as her contribution to the happy day, and righteous good fortune attended to the exterior: the abundant countryside and colourful gardens bathed in warm spring sunshine. Cutting a dashing figure in the conventionality of his morning dress, Hugh was Jack's best man; a girl friend of Lucy's from her school days with Emily's little daughter Isabelle dressed in pink Thai silk were bridesmaids; and little Jules, dressed in a white shirt, light blue silk knickerbocker shorts and lost in bewilderment by the foreign activity of the theatrical occasion, was page boy. The reception was held in a large marquee on the lawn in the gardens at The Nunnery, Jack's parental home, framed by an impenetrable amphitheatre of deep red and white rhododendrons laden with bloom.

As Jack had begun his new job at the start of the year any holiday time allowance for their honeymoon was limited: particularly as he had already made a provisional reservation for them to rent a villa together with Hugh and Belinda for the last two weeks in July. So they decided to return to the conveniently located intimacy of The Family Hotel in Paris for a few days: a present from Lucy's granny.

On their return from honeymoon, the newly weds moved into the apartment as Hugh had moved out. Jack and he had amicably agreed that it had been Jack who had initially found the apartment; it was his signature on the rental contract, and as there were three more years to run, it would be a highly convenient home for them to settle into for the first years of their marriage, before the dependency of children hobbled their independence. Jack and Lucy had been friends and lovers for over a year before their marriage, and nights spent together whenever expedient had revealed to each some unimportant custom for the other's assimilation. But adjustments required for harmony in the daily routines of marriage they soon found, required mutual compromise and gentle immersion. A period of adjustment was necessary. As with all others, they had each grown up in the family confines of their homes and schooling, subject to the moulding of nature or nurture through the influences of genetic inheritance or imposed discipline, and each had grown accustomed to their own ways. Through his upbringing and a strong sense of self reliance imposed on him at boarding school, Jack had an ability to turn his hand to many practical tasks and was orderly in his customary habits - a necessary discipline for two bachelors living in the limited confines of a mini flat – and he had rather taken for granted Lucy's neat and fashionable appearance each time they met: the mystical rituals of female dress and toiletry beyond the boundaries of his male curiosity.

But an innate disorderliness in their wardrobe soon made Jack restive, and pragmatism indicated that Hugh's old bedroom now became Lucy's; not of course for the purpose of passion or sleep, but merely as her private domain in which to keep out of sight the clutter of her clothes, her shoes and the countless creams and cosmetics that crowded the dressing table.

The death of Sir Winston Churchill in January had seemed to mark the end of an era and with it the end of a long established constancy. Traditional deference was increasingly absent between the social classes as well as from the young to their elders, and the bigoted conventions of conservative morality were fast dissolving in the heat of a hedonistic youth culture personified by The Beatles. England was 'swinging' and London was the place to be, with its vibrant music, discotheques and fashion epitomised by The Rolling Stones, Mary Quant and the glaring appeal of Carnaby Street and The King's Road. Uncharacteristically caught up in the thrust of this devil-may-care optimism, Hugh had moved to another flat nearby persuading Belinda to move in with him; his persuasive logic of the importance of prior cohabitation coupled with a hint of marriage overriding her concern of parental discovery.

For the first couple of months following their wedding Jack and Lucy drove down to the countryside most weekends through force of habit, as if reluctant to assume wholeheartedly the independent state of marriage, or subliminally to touch the talismanic stone of parental guidance. Before their marriage each had stayed at their parents' home; the absence of scrutiny during the week rectified by the conventions of social hypocrisy at night each weekend. But now they visited as a couple, endeavouring to alternate their weekend stays whenever they came down between their two sets of parents; initially self conscious in the open legitimacy of their union.

"It's silly I know," Lucy giggled in the bedroom on their first night's stay at her parents' home after their honeymoon, "I feel as if I'm doing something naughty, and my daddy will be very cross if he catches me." She mimicked in a child like voice.

"Well I hope your daddy remembers that we are married. It would be seriously embarrassing if he suddenly burst in at a critical moment." Jack said with mock concern.

"Oh God how dreadful, can you imagine?" Lucy laughed helplessly falling backwards onto the bed. "You with your bare bum in the air and me prostrate underneath."

"Maybe a big turn on." Jack chuckled mischievously. "Do you think these old people still do it?"

"They're not that old," Lucy protested, but frankly I'd rather not think about it."

"Good idea, and changing the subject, we should invite Hugh and Belinda down one weekend when we're staying at The Nunnery. My parents have plenty of room there and we really need to talk over with them our villa rental plan for the summer, so that we can confirm the booking."

"Are they still up for it?"

"Yes certainly as far as I know. I mentioned it briefly when I called Hugh last week and he seemed as keen as ever. His cohabitation with Belinda is going smoothly. The good news is that apparently her parents now know all about them living together, and are perfectly happy with the situation."

"Very *avant-garde*." Do you think your folk would allow them to share a room if they do come down for a weekend?"

"Yes I'm sure I can talk them into it, particularly if I inform them that Belinda's parents are all in favour of the benefits of their trial marriage. With my mother I have the feeling there has never really been a problem - I'm sure she herself was quite a wild one in her day - and maybe now my father has also learned that times have changed after my brief encounter with Mr. Follet on that subject." Jack scoffed, breaking into song with 'England Swings like a Pendulum Do'.

In the months following Jack's resignation from the printing company, a discernible change for the better had appeared in his relationship with his father. The detached formality of corporation chairman, which Harold had felt necessary to adopt within the confines of their offices, had too easily percolated into their family life at home. Now rested in the knowledge that there no longer existed any familial element within the company that could prove an embarrassing liability, he became more at ease, contentedly socialising with the Donaldsons, and taking a particular shine to his daughter-in-law Lucy.

"You're a very lucky young man." He curiously commented to Jack one evening after a couple of whiskies. "If I were thirty years younger I would compete with you for that one." He chuckled mischievously.

"Dad you're just a dirty old man with wishful thinking." Jack countered laughing to dismiss the questionable proposition from his mind. It was not the first time since he had introduced Lucy that his father had shown a mild envy for his son's youth; casual remarks camouflaged by their humorous delivery.

When Jack requested that Hugh and Belinda join them for a weekend at The Nunnery to his surprise there was no objection; Harold and Phyllis were happily agreeable to the idea. Initially he had been concerned that he should couch his words carefully when explaining their living arrangements, but like the salesman that he was he had planned his strategy, casually mentioning the possibility to his mother a couple of weeks before the planned date, knowing his mother would talk it over with his father, smoothing out any potential dissent. Harold and Phyllis had known Hugh as a young friend of Jack's at boarding school, and on the many occasions they had met since the two boys had started their careers, Harold had related to him with familiar ease, naturally comfortable in their similar dispositions. On the day of his wedding Harold had mentioned to Jack of having had an interesting talk with Hugh about business. But aware now with amused endearment of his father's reinvigorated libido, maybe, Jack thought, smiling inwardly as the image crossed his mind: the business was more to do with desire, and the interest more in Belinda standing by his side. Of course Harold had agreed to Hugh and Belinda sharing a room over the weekend he now realised, smiling at the revelation: his father would have the stimulus of two attractive young women in the house. The thought set Jack's mind wandering back to Jenny's strip club, and the clientele with whom he had come to have a nodding acquaintance through the frequency of his visits: an anonymous mixture of unfortunates unblessed by nature, and others of his father's age seeking renaissance; the potency of their love's lust lost, dulled to extinction over years in the repetitive conformity of marriage.

As football fever gripped the country during the summer with England hosting the World Cup, Jack couldn't wait to escape from the inescapable monotony of the subject dominating the media daily; the mind numbing concentration of its detailed analysis seeped inextricably into every conversation. The day before they set off for France by car, Hugh and Belinda came down to The Nunnery again in order that they all could leave together early the following morning. Since losing a company car with his change of job, Jack had copied Hugh and bought an Austin Mini for the convenience of its size parking in London. They had booked with British United Air Ferries for them and the cars to be flown across the Channel from Lydd on the Kent coast to Le Touquet; a quick crossing would enable them to get as far down to their goal as possible for their overnight stay on route. Despite the temptation of the hundreds of miles of the new Autoroute du Soleil motorway, Jack had promised his mother there would be no racing or games.

By the evening of that same day, having stopped for lunch, they comfortably reached south of Valence where they spent their first night in a small hotel in Loriol sur Drome. Jack was animated, he loved coming to France where he had come often as a boy on family holidays with Emily. Going 'to the Continent' with his parents then had been quite an adventure he recalled, his father cautiously driving his beloved Jaguar, having arranged months in advance that their whole trip be carefully studied and planned in detail by the Automobile Association, with all routes determined, detailed road maps supplied and hotels booked. As an added precaution, Harold would check the car's oil and water levels before departure each day; nothing must be left to chance.

Nearing their destination the next day they wound

their way through the dense oak and chestnut woodlands that blanket the hills behind the coast, the intense heat of the day cooled only by the motion of the car and the sweet heady aroma of the Mediterranean air rushing through the windows: hints of wild thyme, pine and olive baked by the sun mingled with salt breezes wafting in from the sea. It was a scent stored in Jack's memory since first coming to the South of France in his teens by overnight train from Paris with his mother and sister, an evocative scent igniting nostalgia, heralding the close proximity of their destination and welcoming their arrival.

"I can see the sea, I can see the sea." Lucy chanted excitedly like a little girl on an outing as they descended to the coast; a breathtaking vista of azure blue sea glinting in the sunlight opening up before their eyes dotted with the sails of yachts little and large. She stuck her arm out of the window pointing ahead to alert Hugh in the car behind, as if the panorama could be overlooked and required emphasis.

"Rather more exhilarating than Brighton wouldn't you agree?" Jack remarked ironically. "The one problem of coming down here for a holiday is that it's so traumatic to go back. There's something vaguely masochistic about it," he laughed, "one dabbles in the blue skied warmth of heaven for a couple of weeks, knowing one must inevitably return to the cold grey damp of hell."

"I thought hell was rather on the warm side." Lucy

giggled.

"That's what they say. I hope I never have to test the theory." Jack replied dryly.

In Sainte Maxime and finding the villa rental office, Lucy volunteered to remain to complete the formalities while the others escaped to stretch their legs and enjoy a beer before being escorted to the house. Set in pinewoods on a hill overlooking the town and glimpses of the sea in the distance, the paint peeling shutters and faded façades of the single story building exuded a dull fundamentality in keeping with the basic requirements of its rental function: an income provider absent of homely occupation. Cicadas buzzed their relentless chorus from the pine trees, but there were no flowers or gardens to attend in the monotonous simplicity of its exterior surroundings, only the earth under a carpet of pine needles. In the interior terrazzo tiles covered the floors throughout, with small rugs positioned in convenient spots such as bedsides to cushion feet, net curtains hung wearily at all the windows, and an assortment of arbitrarily placed impressionist prints decorated the walls. A mélange of stale smells hung in the warm, torpid air. A small sofa of burgundy coloured leatherette and two matching arm chairs sat composed before a tile fronted fireplace offering basic comfort in the sitting room, together with a round high gloss veneer dining table on an ornately carved central support with a matching suite of six erect chairs. In the kitchen, a white enamelled gas cooking stove with a filter coffee pot and a limited selection of cooking pans, utensils, cutlery, glasses, plates, cups and saucers allowed for self catering. A small red Formica topped table with chrome legs and four complementary chairs provided for breakfast. One bathroom with basin, loo, bidet and in-bath shower behind a plastic curtain of tropical fish presaged problems at times of coincidental need.

"Well this is all very nice." Belinda commented ironically after the agent had left. "A little on the fundamental side perhaps, but we're not going to be spending much time here I suppose, only sleeping, so I'm sure it'll be fine."

"Cup half full, that's what I like, but I'm not sure about the sleeping bit. You'll have to negotiate with Hugh about that." Jack teased.

"There are three bedrooms each with two beds, so I suggest we choose or toss for it if we both want the same one." Hugh suggested.

"Yes, and we can keep the other room free for sulking should anyone have need." Jack agreed.

"What happens if two sulkers coincide?" Lucy speculated.

"Then it could get interesting," Jack responded in a suggestive tone, "but let's not go there now. It's a little late for the beach and such so let's just be positive and unpack. Later we can go back into town before the shops close. We have to buy coffee, tea, milk and all else we might need for breakfast, and maybe a bottle of wine or two. I suggest each of us chip an equal sum into a housekeeping budget for now. Either Lucy or Belinda can act as mummy. When and if we need more we can repeat the exercise."

In the early evening they drove back down into town in one car to find a store and the nearest bread shop where they could buy the *baguettes* for breakfast each morning. They strolled along the sea front road to acquaint themselves with its facilities, passing tourist shops, cafés, bars and restaurants, subconsciously noting those whose ambient appeal might attract their custom.

"Well that looks about it." Jack said as they neared the end of the front line and stopped to consult. "Any ideas?"

"I liked the look of that little café with the yellow sunshades." Lucy offered. "I think it was about the only one that didn't have a crowd inside grouped around a television set blaring out the damned World Cup football. Even down here one can't get away from it."

They all agreed and returned, sitting at a table looking out to sea over the road; the boys ordered beers and the girls 'Pernod'.

"Strange isn't it." Lucy commented. "I picked up a taste for 'Pernod' when I was in Paris as an au pair, but I would never think of asking for one in England."

"I like the taste of aniseed." Belinda agreed. "It wouldn't

occur to me in England either, but you know.....when in Rome."

"I'm glad we all so easily agreed on this place." Jack commented as the drinks were served. "Group decisions on holiday can so easily become a basis for dissent don't you think? Of course we must try out new places - and we don't always have to stick together I suppose - but I find so often it's a good plan to discover a favourite spot, a bar, a café and particularly a restaurant, and return there regularly, so that one becomes recognised and a friendly informality can develop: at times of over demand it can greatly help to get a table, jump the queue." He laughed.

"We must not forget that the French eat early." Lucy warned.

"Did anyone spot that little fish restaurant?" Belinda asked pointing up the front road from where they had just returned. "I think it was called '*Chez Langouste*'. It had tables out on a street-side terrace under a large brick red awning. It looked fun and there were people already eating there, locals too by the sound of their conversation which is a good sign. These pavement cafés and restaurants are so attractively French, so *typique*. We're here in the Mediterranean so we should enjoy some delicious *Bouillabaisse* or *Soupe de Poisson*." She suggested enthusiastically.

"Belinda." Lucy said in a mildly accusatory tone. "I think you've been hiding your light under a bushel. Your accent is so good. *Tu peut parler français?*" She asked.

"Just a little." Belinda replied blushing a little at the unexpected attention. "My grandmother on my mother's side came from Carpentras in southern France – you may have seen the signposts after we passed Orange - so I should be fluent I suppose, but unfortunately I'm not."

"Well I don't know about lights and bushels, but it's probably the effects of the

Pernod, it brings out the French in all of us." Jack chuckled. Now we know where you got that jet black hair, dark brown eyes, olive skin and sexy voice."

Hugh looked ill at ease. "Belinda's really whetted my appetite now. Unless anyone's got a much better idea let's drink up and go there, *Chez* whatever, sounds good to me." He suggested.

They were all late waking the following morning, the natural habit of youth when unpressured, stoked by the latent effects of their two day drive and a couple of bottles of Beaujolais with dinner. Semi comatose, each had shuffled successively bleary eyed to the kitchen in their night clothes on getting up, drawn to the constrained tones of familiar voices gathering in unfamiliar circumstances. Jack was the last to appear.

"Good morning all." he muttered. "I desperately need a coffee. It was fun last night and the food was delicious, but my head is telling me the Beaujolais was a bit rough."

"You're in luck it's made already, over there." Lucy indicated. "Belinda was the first up and had the presence of mind to brew the coffee."

"Belinda I love you." Jack said expansively. You're a saviour, a Florence Nightingale for those of us who tend to over do it."

"It's a bit early for declarations of love isn't it?" Lucy suggested.

Jack looked at his watch. "Ten forty two. Frankly I can't think of a better time, especially when induced by the amorous gift of a cup of coffee."

"Jack you're impossible." Belinda responded dismissively with mock disapproval.

"To be serious for a moment - and I hate to break up this love fest - but I suppose one of us has to go down to get a couple of *baguettes*." Hugh interjected. "Why don't you come with me Belinda?"

"OK, just let me throw some clothes on and I'll be with you."

"Try also to get some croissants." Lucy shouted as they were leaving. "If you can't get four get none at all, or somebody will lose out and throw a moody."

After they had left the house Lucy turned to Jack. "I know you're only joking Jack, but I think you should tone down your salesman's charm with Belinda. Don't get the wrong idea," she insisted, "it's really not for me, but I rather get the impression from Hugh's demeanour that he's uncomfortable with your attention to her. He was pretty quiet at dinner last night. I think that was after your sexy voice comment, and all the attention we got from the young waiter didn't help."

"I thought the waiter was great. I loved his *franglais*. If it takes the company of a couple of gorgeous young women to get really good service I'm in." Jack laughed enthusiastically. "Listen, Hugh and I have been close friends for many years. He knows me and my bullshit I can't believe he would take me seriously."

"It's not that he takes you seriously as competition – Jack we're married for God's sake – it's just that you tend to hog the limelight, and by being Mr. Big Personality you may make him look rather dull."

"Hugh's not dull at all, he may not be a great conversationalist, but he's a clever chap and doing rather well actually. But I get your point and I'll try to behave myself." He said in a small voice of mock contrition.

A palpable change of mood pervaded the kitchen when Hugh and Belinda returned with the *baguettes*; no words passed between them. While she applied purposeful attention to the preparation of breakfast, her superficial air of nonchalance betraying a pent up anger of injustice, he confined himself aimlessly to the outer limits of the room: withdrawn, reflective, avoiding enquiry.

"What plans do you have for today Hugh….beach?" Jack asked over the breakfast table anxious to draw him out of his well of self reflection. "We'll be expected to return home bronzed and beautiful, so we'd better put in the hours."

"You make it sound like hard work." Lucy commented.

"Well it is hard work, laughable really, covering one's body with all that oil just to develop an enviable tan for the short period it can remain under the grey skies of home.

In the heat of the sun I feel like a joint of pork salted and oiled to go crispy in the oven. Frankly I can't stand the stuff. If one lies down the sand sticks to it, and if one sits the sand gets up one's arse." Jack laughed.

"The good news for you today Jack is that the beach I saw here in Sainte Maxime is a pebble beach. It won't help with your aversion to oil, but it may save your arse."

Belinda giggled.

Lucy broke into peels of laughter. "It would not be the first time something or somebody has saved his arse eh Jack?" She teased.

Noticeably relieved by the change of mood and Belinda's laughter, Hugh relaxed. "OK let's settle for the local beach today while we're getting acquainted with the area. We could stop at the store on the way down and get a few things for a picnic. It'll be midday before we get going now, and I don't think our budgets will stretch to restaurants for lunch and dinner every day."

"Good idea Hugh." Jack encouraged. "Another day we can explore, go around the bay to Saint Tropez, call in on Bridget Bardot. We've also got the two cars, so if you and Belinda want to be independent anytime, that's fine too with us."

They finished breakfast, the recuperation of their conversation intermittently broken by the silence of indulgence, and the ums and ahs of appreciation for the deliciousness of the croissants, baguettes, butter and apricot jam washed down with deep cups of coffee.

"Don't you just love *croissants* and *baguettes*." Jack asked rhetorically pushing his chair back expansively to extend his legs under the table and lighting a cigarette. "No other country seems to have mastered the culinary secrets of croissants or the humble French *baguette*. They sure expose the tasteless, soggy English cut loaf for what it is: soggy and tasteless in keeping with our weather."

Hugh sloped off leaving little doubt as to the necessity of his destination, while Lucy cleared the table systematically supplying items to Belinda washing up. "Very discerning Jack and surely an important subject we may later debate," she chided ironically, crisscrossing the room, "but right now I really think you should stub out that cigarette and get on with it if we're ever going anywhere today. So please get off your backside and make yourself useful, or at least get dressed."

At the beach determined sunbathers lay on their backs on towels glistening, oiled and motionless, systematically turning as if controlled by timers. A few babies sat at the water's edge mesmerised by the gentle ebb and flow as their young mothers hovered protectively overhead, attentive to those striding by. Teenage locals on holiday chatted in small groups, spontaneously breaking apart with muffled screams as one chased another; boys provoking girls to get attention. In the heated midday haze over the sea, couples on pedalos aimlessly navigated the outer reaches, while others swam purposefully, paddled or played in the shallows throwing balls. With their backs close to the wall along the road a few lightly clothed old couples sat in deck chairs, silently watching and recalling times gone by. Jack strode ahead steering a path between the prostrate bodies, the others following like coolies in the wake of an adventurer. He found a suitable area where they set themselves up, laying beach mats on the pebbles with their possessions on top, as if pioneers making claim to a patch of land.

"I'll oil you Jack and then you can oil me." Lucy suggested.

"No I'm going in for a swim first. It's pointless to oil before."

"We shouldn't all swim at the same time." Hugh advised. "At least one of us should remain here to keep an eye on our things."

"Good point Hugh." Jack agreed. "Why don't you three oil up while I take a quick dip and then I'll stay here to keep an eye."

"Yes." Lucy said with a deep tone of suspicion. "But to keep an eye on what?" she asked, knowingly looking around at the gleaming tanned bodies of all the lithe young women on the beach. "I know you too well Jack Strange." She giggled.

"There's no justice here your honour." Jack protested with mock theatricality. "I'm condemned before any evidence has been presented. OK Lucy, to prove my total innocence we'll take it in turns if Hugh and Belinda agree. They swim now and then we'll swap over."

As Belinda removed her T-shirt and shorts revealing herself in her bikini Jack watched surreptitiously, pleasantly aware of the irony that, had beach been bedroom and bikini bra and panties, the arousal of this intimacy would have been disallowed. Since denying Hugh the exploration of her hidden treasures by returning early from the country that weekend and first meeting Belinda re-buttoning her blouse, he had assumed her gamin appearance concealed a boyish physique. But now he was intent, alerted by the firm, full breasted woman that had emerged; an exotic butterfly from its chrysalis. He sat upright knees bent casually looking to the distance, pretending by his adopted indifference to be oblivious to what had been so tantalisingly revealed; the attraction of her Mediterranean complexion and husky voice now made more evocative by the beautiful, contradictory proportions of her slim young body.

"OK we'll see you." Hugh said as they set off gingerly over the hot pebbles. "You

had better put on some oil or protection Jack, you told us you loathe the stuff, but this sun is very hot, and with your fair skin, you don't want to burn or it'll ruin your holiday."

Hugh's voice seeped into Jack's mind, the mundane message drawing him back into reality from the imaginings of his voyeuristic reverie, and helping to restrain the arousal concealed in his trunks.

"Hugh's right." Lucy said. "Stand up Jack and I'll put this cream on you as you don't like oil."

Jack delayed, things were calming, but required another minute or so. "Darling can't you do that after we've been in the water?"

"No Jack you're already looking a bit red over your shoulders. Stand up please it's easier."

Jack stood, relaxed now that the swelling in his trunks had subsided. "You'd better not make your application of that cream too sensuous or the stimulation may get me all excited." He laughed, unsure nothing remained discernible and creating an excuse if it was.

"Belinda's a good looking girl don't you think?" Lucy asked.

"Yes." Jack agreed artlessly, unsure if the question was loaded, provoked by the unnatural silence of his distraction, and aware that feigned disinterest may only exacerbate suspicion.

"Oh that was wonderful, the sea's so warm." Belinda announced enthusiastically when they returned, dripping water as she reached for her towel.

"Everything all right?" Hugh enquired.

"Well no not really." Jack responded. "Lucy and I were so deeply involved we didn't notice that some bastard must have crept up and walked off with your camera."

"You're kidding?" Hugh exclaimed with indignation.

"Yes of course I am." Jack laughed seeing the concern on Hugh's face. "Come on Lucy it's our turn now."

Jack grabbed Lucy's hand as they hobbled hastily over the hot pebbles, then running through the shallows and plunging into the warm water. After swimming energetically close together for the first few moments, they slowed and stopped, made breathless by the unaccustomed physical exertion. Kicking down their legs to remain afloat they came back close together face to face, she wrapping her arms around his neck her legs around his waist and they kissed passionately. No words passed between them. Each knew what they wanted. Jack gently paddled his legs closer to shore until his toes touched the sea bed to stop them from drifting. Lucy could feel the stiff shaft of his erection protruding from the side of his trunks pressing firmly against her, and taking an arm from around his neck she edged aside the crotch of her bikini, steering him gently up into her. They kissed, no action was necessary as she felt the warmth of his ejaculation flooding into her. For a moment they remained clung together, each mutely savouring the carnal gratification of their clandestine intimacy and the assimilation of a sublime experience.

"Wow! Well that was a new experience." Lucy giggled breaking the spell as she gently released herself from Jack. "One never knows what's in store going for a swim."

"There's got to be a first time for everything. I suppose we'd better swim back slowly and deny everything in case we've been watched." He suggested.

"Well you too love birds rather stuck together." Hugh commented on their return.

"After our initial burst of energy Lucy got cramps in her legs so I had to hold her up until it subsided." Jack answered in a matter of fact tone. Naturally I had to comfort her, so I tried taking her mind off the pain by kissing her passionately. It seemed to work wonders. I really must stick close to her when swimming. It could so easily happen again….. with luck." He chuckled.

"Now your back, Hugh and I are going for a stroll along the sea's edge. Not so satisfying as having cramps, but maybe better exercise." Belinda said knowingly.

"Don't be long?" Lucy said. "We shouldn't have too much sun our first day."

As one lazy sun filled day seamlessly melted into another their time passed: late breakfasts; hours at the beach; people watching with evening aperitifs; animated conversations over dinner in a variety of restaurants; and well intentioned plans for exploring the coast and hinterland abandoned: enthusiasm drained in the summer heat.

Late one night after dinner strolling through the streets and drawn by the sound of pulsing music blaring from somewhere deep beneath, they found *Le Caveau*. Hesitantly descending the staircase, they entered a dimly lit space packed with an animated crowd engrossed in lively conversations at tables surrounding a small dance floor bursting with contorted action. Spotlights illuminated the central scene through a cloud of cigarette smoke. Barely discernable through the hazy glare, a small live band in the shadows blasted out their rhythm, each player enveloped in their own intoxication. A couple of waitresses miraculously supporting trays packed with glasses high above their heads wove amongst the tables.

"Wow this is great let's see if we can grab a table." Jack enthused moving further into the seething den.

"Don't worry about a table Jack let's dance." Lucy yelled over the din, simultaneously leaping into the mêlée with Belinda close behind.

"Come on boys." Belinda shouted seductively.

Propelled by the exhilaration of the moment Jack hurled himself onto the dance floor uninhibitedly, and Hugh followed cautiously hovering on the outer rim, self conscious in his inability. Remorselessly the pounding beat of the music continued unabated as if on a loop, a relentless battle to a standstill between the band and those on the floor. Soon Hugh dropped out and gradually others too surrendered leaving Lucy, Jack and Belinda gyrating alone. And then the band stopped, allowing only the crazed drummer to continue to pound solo with increased frenzy the battery of drums and cymbals grouped around him. Jack signalled his fatigue to Lucy, and like two clockwork toys with their springs unwound, they petered out and moved aside expecting Belinda to join them but she stayed. Imperceptibly the level of conversation in the room faded as the crowd became aware of the unfolding scene: Belinda, centred, spotlighted, alone, hypnotised by the tribal beat of the drums, oblivious to all around her as she danced with the abandoned ardour of a voodoo spell. Jack stood in silent awe, entranced by the sensuousness of the primal spectacle before his eyes, the lure of Belinda's tight body, the teasing incitement of her mini skirt, and breasts pulsating in the strained tension of her sweat soaked T-shirt. Suddenly the drummer stood erect from his stool and crashed across his drums with exhaustion. A gasp rose in the room, and in the moment of imposed silence Belinda ground to a halt as if awakening from a dream, or the plug had been pulled from the source of her energy. The crowd broke into spontaneous applause. Hugh crossed the floor and put his arm around her and she walked off diffidently, deceptively unaware of the constrained arousal she had generated in every man in the room.

Drawn by the illusion of jet set glitterati one day they ventured around the bay to Saint Tropez, strolling through the narrow streets enticed by the novelty of the shops, cafés, bars and innumerable restaurants before opening onto the wide quay overlooking the harbour. In the late afternoon sun they found a vacant table under the welcome shade of the red awning at *Sénéquier*. Content to sip, watch and comment, eyes alert to recognise the recognisable they remained entranced, captivated by the quarter deck activities on the huddle of sleek, tall-masted sailing yachts moored side-by-side against the quayside in front, and the pageant of curious characters passing by.

"I could sit here all day and remain entertained." Jack commented. "It's like watching an ongoing show for the cost of a few rounds of drinks."

"Well we have been here almost a couple of hours already. What's the plan?" Hugh asked. "I'm getting rather peckish. If we leave it too long all the restaurants will be packed. Let's move on soon and scout around the old town for a place for dinner?"

They set off into the maze of quaint cobbled alleyways of the old fishing port rising up behind the quay, and settled on one of the many small restaurants already bustling with custom; enticed by the appetising aromas and tempting dishes being consumed on the open terrace. Taking the initiative and judging which of the busy waiters may be the boss, Jack asked for a table on the terrace.

"*Vous avez une reservation monsieur*?" The waiter asked with a haughty tone of prejudged finality.

Recalling the same question in an empty restaurant in Montmartre, Jack edged Lucy forward. "No *monsieur*, but I have two beautiful young women." He laughed.

The waiter glanced at Lucy and Belinda: silent, unimpressed. "*Bon. S'il vous plait.*" He announced decisively guiding them stylishly to a vacant table.

"That was a spot of luck." Lucy said as they sat down.

"You can say that again." Jack laughed. "I had the impression it would have carried more weight if I had been able to say I had a couple of handsome young men."

As the evening sun faded into twilight and darkness they indulged themselves more as their wine consumption increased, their mood and conversation exhilarated by the carefree detachment of being young and on holiday. Freed from the boring actuality of the mundane and ever more expansive in the comradely ambience of their surroundings, they came to perceive by the existential reality of their presence, the memorable gratification of belonging. A photographer passed among the tables snapping snaps and giving his card to those interested. Jack beckoned him over and they grouped themselves as a foursome, arms around each others shoulders: it was a moment captured, then unimportant, to be valued more in the years ahead.

Chapter 5
No Room For Guilt

Less than two months after their return to London Jack had bedded Belinda - or Belinda had bedded Jack - commensurate with either one's point of view. Bland conversation in the sweaty aftermath on crumpled sheets absolved love of any responsibility, merely the unbridled lust of one, a need for passion in the other, and the convenience of a mutual absence of guilt. By chance Jack had bumped into Belinda on the Brompton Road in front of Harrods, his mind intent on the task in hand he had not spotted Belinda on the crowded pavement walking towards him.

"Jack!" He heard a familiar voice exclaim.

Diverting his attention from the shop front windows he looked ahead. "Belinda. Good to see you. You're looking great as usual. You know I had a feeling when I woke this morning that there was something exceptional about today, and here you are." he laughed.

"Jack you're so full of bullshit, but I do love you for it."

She chuckled. "How's Lucy?"

"Lucy's fine, thank you. She has a birthday coming up at the end of the month, so I'm playing truant from my job seeking a suitable present."

"Oh is she a Virgo?"

"No she's Libra……very balanced, not like me, I'm a Virgo."

"It's quite difficult to imagine you were ever a virgin." Belinda laughed teasingly.

"I'm not sure that's fair, but I see my reputation goes before me." He said with a broad smile. "What are you doing in this neck of the woods?"

"You know I work as a temporary secretary and I'm between jobs at the moment. My parents keep a London pad in Beaufort Gardens for family convenience when they're up in town. I keep an eye on it for them from time to time; collect any post and open the windows to air the place. I'm on the way there now."

"You said family convenience. Do you have brothers or sisters, I've never asked?"

"Yes I have an older sister Charlotte. She's married with two little kids. I'm an aunt." She giggled. "Her husband is a doctor. They live in an old rectory in the village of Zeals. You look blank, which is understandable. It's in Wiltshire, near Warminster."

"Oh. Are your parents up in town now?"

"No." she replied coquettishly. "By the way, must you find that present today or have you time for a coffee? It's just round the corner."

Jack smiled knowingly as if in mild reproach. "My head is telling me firmly to concentrate on shopping, but on the other hand," he paused, "well on the other hand I do rather like the idea of coffee."

Constrained anticipation hung in the air as Belinda showed Jack around the first floor apartment: the small kitchen where she put on the kettle, the bathroom, her parents' bedroom, the guest bedroom, and a spacious sitting room traditionally decorated with a comfortable sofa, armchairs, oriental carpets and various fine pieces of antique furniture covered with family photographs in silver frames. A large gilt mirror hung over the fireplace, and two landscape paintings in gilt frames on the opposing wall. Elegant floral patterned chintz curtains with matching pelmets in the form of swags, framed French windows opening onto a narrow balcony looking into the trees in the square below.

"Well this is very attractive, and useful one might say." Jack commented as they went back into the kitchen.

"Useful?" Belinda asked. "That's an odd compliment."

"Well it's very conveniently located......I mean for your parents when they're up in town." Jack clarified; giving her a knowing smile and lighting a cigarette.

"How do you take your coffee?" Belinda asked pouring the hot water into the mug. "I suppose I should know from our days on holiday, but I've forgotten, that is if I ever paid attention in the first place."

"Well I recall you take yours with milk and one teaspoon of sugar." Jack responded.

"Very observant, but that wasn't all I noticed you observing Jack Strange." she said accusingly.

"Really I have no idea what you're talking about." Jack responded with mock indignation.

"You may have thought I didn't notice you eying me taking my clothes off on the beach that first day at Sainte Maxime, but I did." She said in a tone of feigned accusation. "Actually I have to say I rather enjoyed it, quite turned me on. I know it really turned you on, I watched you with Lucy doing it in the sea."

Jack felt his arousal. "No healthy male would be surprised." He said taking off his jacket and coming closer. "You appear clothed as this petite young woman. Nobody would suspect that concealed underneath is a fabulous lithe figure and surprisingly firm, large breasts."

"Maybe you'd better get to know me better." She responded suggestively, taking his hand and drawing him towards the guest bedroom.

"Are you sure you want to do this?" Jack asked.

"Jack if I hadn't thought long and hard about it….if

you'll excuse the expression," she giggled. "I would not have risked inviting you for coffee."

"I just need to be sure; we don't want any later recriminations. You're on the pill?"

"Yes of course I am."

In the bedroom they kissed gently as if the act of kissing was somehow a necessary expression of affection, a social password, a precursor to the purely carnal intent of their physical desire. Unzipping his trouser she released his stiff swelling massaging it gently while he loosened the buttons of her jeans putting his hand down into her crotch stimulating her passion. She broke away, impatient to liberate her body from the restriction of her clothes and threw back the bed cover falling back naked onto the sheets, her legs apart over the side. Jack stripped and knelt on the floor gently kissing her pubic mound then stimulating her to ecstasy with his tongue. For a moment Belinda lay still savouring the deluge of emotions running through her body before bending forward and cupping his head between her hands drawing him up onto the bed. For a while they lay side by side, she on her back and Jack supported on one elbow caressing her breasts and running his tongue around the brown perimeters of her hardened nipples. Belinda rose to face him, and Jack, sinking back, gently pushed her head down to his erection. Squatting astride him, Belinda eased down enveloping him up into her with a muffled groan, careful not to provoke a premature ejaculation. At first she rose and fell slowly, her pace steadily increasing as the frenzied torrent of transmissions in her body drove her ever more furiously, miraculously erupting simultaneously in gasps of mutual fulfilment.

For a while they lay still, contemplative, absorbing the rewards of their sensual satisfaction in the pregnant silence. In time Jack's hand wandered over to find the warmth of her groin again, encouraging her through the irresistible temptation of her longing slowly to open her legs to his re-penetration. She lay in abandoned ecstasy with her arms above her head on the pillow as he mounted her drawing back her knees, moaning softly as he teasingly inched in and out the length of his revived erection, her breasts pulsing with the pumping of his steadily increasing rhythm until he came again, falling aside with the exhaustion of his exertion.

In the afterglow they lay silent, each digesting within the privacy of their minds the significance of their actions.

Belinda's voice softly broke the silence. "In case you're lying there in a mute state of guilt and self recrimination Jack, I just want to tell you it was wonderful. Thank you."

"I'm not." Jack replied. "It was very good for me too, in fact I was just wondering how we can arrange to do this more often." He chuckled.

"Really? No regrets?"

"Really. No regrets." Jack repeated assuredly, pausing in thought. "If you don't mind me asking, why did you do it? I mean we both know this is not love, and we both know my reputation, but tell me, what's your excuse?" He laughed.

"Jack I do love Hugh. He's a great guy, honourable, honest, steady and loving with all the potential to be a good husband and father….."

"But?" Jack interjected. "With a list like that there's always a but."

"Well he's very loving, but he's not a lover. There's no passion, no excitement. We make love conventionally to satisfy his need and he gives little attention to mine. You poked Lucy in the sea. The idea would never occur to Hugh; he just goes swimming. Hey, maybe you could give him some lessons." She laughed dropping back onto the pillows.

Compelled by urges of recalled gratification in moments of reflection, Jack and Belinda continued to meet in the same location whenever addictive need necessitated. Instinctively no mention was ever made of the other's partner in their hours of sexual serendipity, as if blinkered from reality they would be spared the unease of percolating guilt. Jack relaxed in the thought that theirs were insignificant interludes of self indulgence devoid of love and divorced from actuality, while Belinda assured herself of their mutual benefit in her life with Hugh: she achieved the libidinous ecstasy she sought from time to time, relieving him from the one aspect of their relationship in which he appeared wanting. Singing along to the Rolling Stones "I Can't Get No Satisfaction," she concluded in private with a giggle "Oh yes I can."

Strolling home through the park from the office in the soft evening sunlight of late spring the following year, his mind drifting aimlessly, Jack stumbled upon the comforting realisation that all was presently going rather well in his life: he loved Lucy, she loved him, soon it would be their first wedding anniversary and thankfully his new job was going well. His suggestion to Bill Harris that they could increase the company's profitability by securing the print contracts for the graphic design work they were handling had proved successful, and brought in new catalogue productions much to his credit. A warm pulse of contentment rippled through his mind; for the time being at least all was going smoothly, under control, nothing particular to worry about.

Prompted by that thought Belinda entered his mind and he resolved to end their meetings. Increasingly he had felt uncomfortably guarded when together with Lucy and Hugh. The irresistible novelty of her body had diminished with familiarity, and the risk of suspicion unjustified by the declining dividends of the adventure. He would call her and tactfully explain, he said to himself, confident that she would understand.

"But Jack it's not as easy as that." Belinda said with a

disconcerting smile after he had gently explained the logic of his reasoning, convinced of his proven salesmanship.

It was not the reaction Jack anticipated and he felt a twinge of irritation. From his point of view, it had always been clearly understood that theirs was a mutually selfish relationship purely based on sexual gratification – if purely was a word that could be associated with their licentious activities. They were not in love, they never had been in love; with all its agonies and ecstasies, the stomach churning insecurities and selfless devotion that that state of emotion demanded, only to risk the lacerating hurt of rejection in favour of another.

"I never said it was easy," Jack objected, "but it's the right way to go. The longer we go on seeing each other illicitly somebody is going to find out and the pain we will have caused will be unredeemable."

"Jack I'm pregnant." Belinda said with concerned seriousness.

"What!" Jack exclaimed loudly, a myriad of emotions expressed in his face. "How do you know? No forget that, it's rather a stupid question. What I mean is how do you know it's mine?"

"I didn't say it is yours, I just wanted to enjoy the shock on your face." Belinda giggled. Anyway I'm not pregnant so you can relax." She hurriedly added.

The relief on Jack's face spoke a thousand words but

all he said was "Thank God for that. For a minute there Belinda you truly had me fooled, but let's face it, if you were pregnant, the ramifications would have been rather unthinkable." He laughed nervously.

"Well I couldn't just let you get away with it too easily Jack Strange. I know you pride yourself on your considerable powers of persuasion, and I really do appreciate your smooth presentation not to offend me, but just for fun I thought I should illustrate that there are circumstances in which even you cannot talk yourself out of."

"How's it going with Hugh?"

"Well, he's asked me to marry him and I've said yes." She answered coyly. "I was going to call you too to say we must stop, but you beat me to it."

"Congratulations, well done, that's fantastic. Hugh hasn't mentioned a word to me about his intentions, so I had better be careful to know nothing when he does. Have you made any plans for a wedding date?"

"No we haven't fixed a date, it's still early days and there's everything yet to arrange, but probably in early autumn. Listen I must go," Belinda said rising and holding out her arms to embrace Jack, "but I just want to say it's been wonderful with you, an experience I will never forget or regret. The good news is that I think I've subtly been able to encourage Hugh to be, let's just say, 'more adventurous' in bed, so maybe my times of promiscuity are over." Belinda laughed.

"Maybe!?" Jack exclaimed with feigned horror.

"Well you know what they say: never say never." She responded seductively.

Jack enveloped Belinda in his arms pecking her cheek with a kiss. "One for the road?" he murmured suggestively into her ear.

Belinda pushed him away giggling. "Jack Strange you really are impossible." She said with mock condemnation.

Heady memories of last summer's days in the sun on the Côte d'Azur and the disturbing eroticism of their subsequence with Belinda, accentuated the grey skies and wet pavements of London. Jack yearned to get away to the sunshine again but could not afford it. When Hugh suggested he and Lucy should come down to his family home in Wiltshire for the weekend, Jack jumped at the idea.

"I'm taking a long weekend – Thursday through to Tuesday – any chance you could too?" Hugh asked.

"Sounds wonderful, just what I could do with right now." Jack responded, intrigued as to why the sudden invitation. "I've got some holiday owing so I'll see what I can arrange and check with Lucy. If we can make it, with these long evenings of daylight, may I suggest we come down from town late on Thursday evening returning on Monday evening, if that's OK with your parents?"

Hugh's parents, Charles and Sybil Henderson, lived in a beautiful 15th century timber framed manor house surrounded by landscaped gardens, orchards and acres of open fields dotted with small woods a few miles west of the picturesque village of Lacock in Wiltshire. Despite their close friendship Jack had not visited Hugh's home before, but he had been told proudly all about it, seen photographs, and now with his curiosity aroused he was keen to know the property first hand.

"So you haven't seen Hugh's parents since leaving school?" Lucy commented rhetorically as they drove down. "Do you remember them?"

"As you know Hugh is an only child like you. His parents married quite late in life.

I recall his father being an imposing man: tall, slim, dark haired and impeccably dressed. He had a beak nose and exuded an authority which I must say I found rather unnerving as a boy; one of those knowing looks that made one feel guilty even though innocent. In my mind's eye I can see now just how like his father Hugh has become in many ways."

"He sounds rather Dickensian." Lucy giggled. "What about his mother?"

"She was always affectionate I remember, but she too had an air of no nonsense about her." Jack chuckled. "She was also quite tall, brown haired and conservatively dressed in tweed suits, twin sets, pearls and sensible shoes, you know, the epitome of a dominant figure engaged in local affairs: Women's Institute, good works."

"She too sounds rather formidable I hope they've mellowed with time. It's a little strange that Hugh has never invited you down to his home in all these years?"

"Well in all honesty I think he may have mentioned it in the early years after leaving school, but probably I did not pursue the idea remembering just how, as you put it 'Dickensian' I recalled his parents being. Recently Hugh told me his father had taken partial retirement from his firm of stockbrokers Henderson, Barnes and Willis in Bath where he had been the senior partner. Maybe this has something to do with our visit."

The warm amber glow of summer's late evening light filtered over the gardens as Jack and Lucy drove up to the house, its rambling form silhouetted against the salmon pink of the setting sun, their tyres crunching to a halt on the gravel. Jack peeped the car horn gently signalling to Hugh their arrival. Shortly the front door opened and a tall figure stood momentarily dark against the light of the interior before moving towards the car.

"A bit late I'm afraid but we made it." Jack called out recognising Hugh.

"Well done. I hope you didn't have too much trouble finding the place, it's easy to get lost around the lanes the first time, but I trust you followed my instructions."

"Naturally: perfect as always Hugh." Lucy responded assuredly giving him a kiss.

They entered into a spacious hall with oriental rugs on a grey flag stoned floor. Limed oak beams crossed the ceiling and appeared exposed in the framed structure of the white painted walls decorated with portraits and landscape paintings. A stand burdened with coats and hats stood over a neat row of boots by the front door, with a large oriental urn crowded with walking sticks and umbrellas. On one side half way down the hall a matching pair of Chinese vases had pride of place amongst other smaller pieces of porcelain on an antique side board. A door to the right was ajar, and Hugh signalled to be quiet, mouthing silently that his father was in the sitting room dosing.

"Mother and Belinda are preparing some supper." Hugh said crossing the hall and entering the large kitchen. "Look whose here." He announced cheerfully.

Belinda looked up with a broad smile holding out her messy hands in explanation of her inability at that moment to embrace. Hugh's mother came around the kitchen island.

"Jack. It's good to see you again." Sybil said giving him a motherly hug. "My you're now quite the man and married too."

"Mummy please don't start saying: I remember you when you were only so old and so high." Hugh laughed.

"And this must be Lucy." Sybil continued enthusiastically, holding her two hands warmly then drawing her into a hug. "Hugh has told us so much about you I feel I know you already."

A movement at the door caught their attention. "What's all this noise? A poor fellow can't even have a nap without being disturbed." Hugh's father demanded with mock irritation as he came in smiling. "Hello young man. Still leading my son astray?" He laughed openly as he greeted Jack warmly. "And this must be Lucy." He continued extending his hand and bending to give her a peck on the cheek. "We've heard so much about you."

"Not all too bad I hope." Lucy asked sweetly with feigned concern.

"Quite the contrary my dear." He responded with the meaningful tone of tender memories recalled.

"Come on Jack I'll show you and Lucy to your room. I'm sure you'll want to freshen up before supper."

They climbed the creaking wooden staircase to the upper floor landing and down a long corridor leading into a spacious guest bedroom the full width of that section of the house directly under the roof. Wide oak boards polished over centuries formed the floor covered in part by a large, colourful kilim rug. Vertical beams exposed in the white walls rose from floor level to another running horizontally at eye level on three sides of the room, and others rose up forming the roof structure, supported on a central joist running the length of the room at its apex. Opposite the door, two curved oak beams arched over from either corner of the wall joining a vertical beam at the centre with a cosily inviting king size bed strewn with cushions; its floral patterned headboard matching the fabric covered bedside tables, lampshades and curtains. On either side of the room the fading evening light filtered in through latticed glass windows. To the right of the door stood a large oak clothes cupboard, and under one window a small antique table and armchair.

"And......you also have the added luxury of an en suite bathroom." Hugh said with pride turning and pushing open the door.

"Oh what a simply beautiful room. What luxury" Lucy exclaimed. "I just adore the pale oak beams silvered with age. It's all so cosy, I love it, I think I'll stay."

"Yes this will do us nicely thank you Hugh, we'll see you in the morning." Jack laughed.

"OK I'll tell mother you won't be down for supper. By the way we're having roast lamb, mint sauce, red currant jelly, roast potatoes, broccoli, peas and gravy followed by sherry trifle. Oh, and I think father will open a couple of bottles of Bordeaux too."

"Sold." Jack pronounced. "Sounds delicious, we'll be down in a minute."

"What would you like to drink before dinner? I'll have it waiting for you when you come down." Hugh asked.

"Two gin and tonics please Jeeves."

"OK but don't be too long, I know you Jack, when you're alone in a bedroom with an attractive woman."

Although he could not think of a subject or matter of potential concern that could have generated this kind but curious invitation for the weekend, Jack remained attentive throughout the evening's conversation for any hint of an answer but none came. And perhaps there was none he thought. Sitting at the table consciously charming his hosts with humorous recollections of past times in banter with Hugh, he smiled inwardly as he imagined the scene and characters around the table as being in an Agatha Christie play; alert for a slip that would reveal all. Conversation drifted through current events: generational exchanges over differing opinions on the situation in Rhodesia, the convenience of the recently launched Barclay Card predicting a future cash free society, and the extraordinary novelty of an English safari park within the county at Longleat, provoking Belinda's concern that lions may escape. Lulled by the wine, the meal and the hour, Jack reflected on the passage of time since he had last seen Hugh's parents as a school boy. They were vigorous then but now grey haired; how strange to recall being cowed by their authoritative manner. Time had brought him adulthood and confidence, and time had brought them frailty and vulnerability; the seesaw of life's successive generations; one goes up as the other goes down.

"Well it's time for us old folk to retire to bed." Charles said rising slowly. We'll see you all in the morning.....no hurry though, we know you youngsters like to sleep on. Clear consciences I suppose." He chuckled confident of his irony. "Come on Sybil or they'll drag you into the washing up. Good night."

As they all rose from the table, Hugh and Belinda went to the door to kiss them goodnight. "We'll just clear up and I think we'll all soon be up ourselves." Hugh said.

"What time should we be down for breakfast?" Jack asked as they parted in the corridor on their way to bed.

"I think nine thirty should do it. Despite what he said, Dad's always down quite early. Old habits die hard. He takes mother a cup of tea in bed. I'll give you a knock on your door at nine. Good night."

Aroused by the virgin territory of their bed and the undefiled crispness of freshly laundered sheets, Jack and Lucy made love; slowly, gently, tenderly, the physical expression of a mutually caring affection absent of carnal self gratification. As Jack moved away he noticed tears in her eyes.

"What's the matter darling?" he whispered with concern. "Did I hurt you? Did I say something at dinner to upset you?"

Lucy rolled over putting her arm over him clinging close and burying her face in his side. "No Jack it was wonderful. I pray we will always be together like this."

"Darling you're so sweet and so loving, only we can make sure of that, sleep tight."

Bright light radiating through the curtains penetrated Jack's sleep early the following morning. He tried to return to sleep but could not escape the relentless rotation of trivial thoughts teasing his mind. Reaching over carefully he looked at his watch on the bedside table; it was just before 8.00 am. For a while he lay still with his eyes closed, a mixed bag of images running through his mind. He thought of Belinda asleep beside Hugh in another room nearby, the vulnerability of Lucy's love that night, and in his heart he knew he had betrayed that love and his friend. He shook his head to dismiss the thought, unwilling to bear the burden of a useless spiral of consuming guilt, and feeling the demand of nature's morning habit. Cautiously he slipped out of the bed crossing silently toward the bathroom, and pausing by the window he gently eased back the edge of the curtain, his eyes adjusting to the glare. Oblique sunlight glistened on the morning dew, a grey squirrel skipped across the lawn stopping sporadically to check for danger, and at the end of the garden a pair of plump pheasants pecked for breakfast at the edge of the orchard. Bloody cheek he murmured to himself, sorry not to be at home with his gun. He crept back to the bed and stood looking down at Lucy still asleep, warm and cosy with a childlike innocence, her tussled blonde hair on the pillow, her face buried in the sheet. She stirred, as if aware that she was being watched, and opened her eyes.

"Hello." She said softly.

"Good morning darling."

"Have you been there long staring at me?"

"No. I just went to the loo. I was looking at you asleep and thinking how lucky I am to have such an adorable wife."

"You can't say those things from outside the bed." She giggled.

Invigorated by the fresh new day Jack slipped back into bed gently pushing back the sheet to expose Lucy's breasts and the soft warmth of her naked body. For a moment he leaned on his elbow looking at her as if seeing her for the first time. A surge of passion welled up inside him; a compelling desire to be absorbed into the beauty of her being like melting snow dissolves into the earth. A firm knock on the door said it was 9.00 o'clock.

After breakfast Hugh suggested they go for a walk, and sensing a revelation Jack was enthusiastic for the fresh air and exercise. They crossed the garden and through a small wooden gate entering into a grassy field pimpled with molehills and fringed with hedgerows of hawthorn, ash and hazelnut. Following one behind the other down a narrow footpath, they reached a fence and climbed over a style onto a bridle path banked high on either side with brambles, bracken and rabbit warrens speckled with sunlight through the overhanging trees.

"It's good to see your folk again Hugh." Jack offered as a possible incentive. "I was recalling to myself over dinner last night how unnerved by them I was as a boy. I think in fairness you have to admit they were quite a formidable pair then, but they've mellowed with age. Your mother has been so warm and affectionate, and your father's still very much on the ball, judging by your debate with him last night over Rhodesia."

"Yes I know what you mean." Hugh agreed. "But actually my father is not well."

"Oh Hugh I'm so sorry to hear that. He seems such a dear." Lucy said. "Nothing too serious I hope."

"That's very kind of you Lucy, but I regret to have to say that it is serious, very serious, in fact that's one of the reasons I asked you to come down this weekend. Dad's had a lot of pain in his lower back for some time, and now he's been diagnosed with prostate cancer. The bad news, unfortunately, is that they caught it too late so it has spread into his bones. That's the reason for his extreme pain. It's terminal. He's been given six months to live.

The sudden determination of a precise period of life expectancy, a death penalty for the crime of living, fell like a guillotine on their conversation exposing mute reflection: what would I feel if it were me? It seemed so unreal, out of place on a bright summer's day. In the light of the gravity of the news any expression of condolence appeared inadequate, impotent to ease the pain in the face of its significance. For a moment they walked on in silence each involved in their thoughts. A blackbird, ever vigilant, fled out of the undergrowth before them announcing to all the alarm, and a pair of startled pigeons crashed out from the branches above. Crows roosting on their nests high in the trees of the adjacent woodland cawed out the invulnerability of their altitude, as the crackled burr of a distant harvester appeared to draw nearer and faded again.

"Well that's the bad news, but there is some good news we also want to announce." Hugh said more cheerily to brighten the mood. "At last I have asked Belinda to marry me….."

"And?" Jack interrupted.

"And the really good news is that she has agreed."

"Oh that is such good news." Jack exclaimed accentuating 'such' in his determination to convey its novelty. He stopped and turned, simultaneously gripping his friend's hand and embracing him in a manly hug as heart felt commiseration for the bad news, felicitation for the good. "Congratulations old chap." He said chuckling teasingly and winking at Belinda. "You're depriving the field of one of its sexiest contenders."

"I'm so thrilled for you both." Lucy exclaimed excitedly hugging Belinda. "Silly question I'm sure, but have you thought of a date yet for the wedding?"

"In view of my father's situation it really has to be sooner rather than later. A month has already passed since the fatal diagnosis, and we really don't want him attending his only child's wedding in insufferable pain. Belinda and her family have very kindly agreed that we have the wedding here in our local church on Saturday September 10th so that father will not have the severe discomfort of any jolting in his back travelling down by car to Sherborne. The reception will be at home in a marquee on the lawn. We will invite only immediate family and close friends so that the day doesn't prove too stressful for him, and Jack, I would like you to be my best man. What do you say?"

"Of course Hugh it will be an honour, in fact I'd be bloody furious if you had asked anyone else." He laughed loudly.

"Lucy I would have loved you to be one of my bridesmaids, but I'm told that by tradition, bridesmaids are unmarried." Belinda said. "Apparently that's why the bride throws her bouquet over her shoulder before leaving for her honeymoon. One of the bridesmaids hopes to catch it as a sign that she will be next up at the altar, or any other unmarried hopeful could grab it I suppose." she chuckled.

"Anyway our news for you doesn't end there." Hugh continued as they strolled on. "My father has now retired from his partnership in Bath and proposed to me that I come down to join the firm as a junior partner in order to continue the family name in the firm. I agreed, and in view of the time factor being imposed on us by father's illness, Belinda and I will be making the move down here from London next month during the silly season of August. That will allow us to be here to arrange more easily the wedding, and also to help mother with dad. When he goes, I know it is mother's greatest nightmare that she could be forced to leave the property as it would really be far too large for her to live in and manage on her own, so Belinda and I will take over the property and move in permanently. We have agreed with mother that we will have the larger part of the house on our own in which hopefully we can start a family, and we will have to make some minor alterations to create a smaller self contained accommodation for mother - a granny flat - so that we can be close by to take care of her.

"Well Hugh it's really sad news about your father, but clearly you've been giving the whole situation a lot of thought and have it all well worked out; not that I would have expected anything different. We will certainly miss the convenience of seeing you both so frequently living nearby, but then again, we will have the advantage of a great alternative for our country weekends visiting you down here." Jack said smiling broadly.

"And how about you Belinda, naturally it's very difficult for you both, but how do you feel about the situation, I mean moving out of London down to this part of the world – a country wife and mother soon as well by the sound of it?" Lucy asked.

"Well to be frank it has all come rather out of the blue, and naturally I wish the circumstances could have been different, I mean with Hugh's father, but I have to say I'm thrilled to be marrying Hugh and excited about our futures down here in deepest Wiltshire. At heart I'm a country girl anyway, and it will be good to be much nearer my parents and see more of my sister's family."

"Yes of course. I remember your parents live down near Sherborne," Lucy responded, "but I had forgotten you also have a married sister living down in this neck of the woods, although I'm sure Jack must have told me some time."

"Listening to the efficient clarity of Hugh's plans for your futures, you know, moving to the country, children and so on, makes me realise how very little I have thought about it." Jack said. "Lucy and I might soon have to do the same, I mean think about it, although I have to admit the whole subject of having children and all that that implies brings me out in a cold sweat." He chuckled. "We only have another year or so left on our rental contract, and although that might be renewable, clearly the flat would be far too small to accommodate any additions. I suppose one day maybe we will also be moving to the countryside. I'll just have to jump off that bridge when we come to it." He laughed nervously, glancing at Lucy vainly endeavouring to read her response.

Returning home Hugh requested that no mention be made of his father's illness, only the news of their upcoming wedding. "He would be furious if he knew I had told you, but it was important for me to explain to you the full circumstances regarding the comparative haste of our wedding, and our move down here out of London. I wouldn't want anyone to have got the wrong idea; Belinda's not pregnant." He laughed. "Father's a very private person in that respect, old fashioned perhaps. I can hear him now saying: there are some subjects one just does not talk about – like politics, money and religion."

On the breezy day Hugh and Belinda were married, grey clouds presaging the approach of autumn scudded across the pale blue sky threatening rain but happily none came. Family and friends crowded the ancient village church decked with banks of glorious flowers, and buzzing with the murmured conversation of reunions; social observations and the constrained tones of the organ's melody. Hugh with Jack at his side stood tall and elegant in his morning dress at the top of the nave smiling in recognition of family and friends as they took their seats in the pews behind.

Suddenly the organ blasted out the strains of the wedding march trumpeting the bride's arrival, and the congregation stood. Hugh turned and smiled with awe at the beauty of his bride graciously making her way up the aisle on the arm of her father to stand beside him.

The vicar stood facing the bride and groom with a welcoming smile and addressed the congregation. "We are gathered here today in the sight of God and the presence of friends and loved ones to celebrate one of life's greatest moments, to give recognition to the worth and beauty of love, and to add our best wishes and blessings to the words that shall unite Hugh and Belinda in holy matrimony. Marriage is a most honourable estate created and instituted by God….." the vicar droned on, but Jack was not listening, his thoughts were elsewhere until suddenly caught and drawn back into sharp focus.

"Should there be anyone who has cause why this couple should not be united in marriage they must speak now or forever hold their peace."

In the moment's silence that fell Jack looked across at Belinda, virginal in her white wedding dress, and smiled inwardly at memories of the intimate treasures he knew that lay underneath. Never had he seen her looking so serenely attractive. He considered the significance of the words just spoken by the vicar sensing a twinge of unease that a divine voice of dissent might boom down from the heavens above:

"This bride before you hast lain in passion with the groom's best friend at his side." Angst entered his mind and he felt in his pocket for reassurance that the ring was still there.

Jack and Lucy said their goodbyes to Hugh's parents the following day aware of the sad likelihood that they would not see his father again. Jack had now got to know them on equal terms as an adult, and the thought of the finality of death, that from one day to the other this living, breathing, thinking man would no longer exist, was difficult for him to assimilate. No mention had been made of the gravity of his condition and therefore nothing more could be said other than kind expressions of gratitude and the social hypocrisy of wishing each other well until the next time they meet. In the late hours of the reception Hugh and Belinda had escaped away to their honeymoon in Venice, leaving them with the realisation that they would no longer be living just around the corner on their return. Long bouts of silent reflection filled the hours of their drive back up to London as each reflected on the events, conversations and significance of what had transpired over the weekend; a homesickness for a recent past that would now be forever changed.

Chapter 6
Burden Of Bertrayal

By early autumn two years after their marriage, Hugh and Belinda were well settled and happy in their new lives in rural Wiltshire. Their first child, a boy christened Toby, had celebrated his first birthday that summer, and Belinda was again heavily expectant and weary in the last month of her second pregnancy. The minor works required to create a comfortable self contained apartment for Hugh's mother had soon been completed, and although there had been a natural period of adjustment to her new circumstances, Hugh and Belinda were gratified to see her revitalised by having them living close by, and the constant joy she derived from her first grandchild. Each day of the working week Hugh commuted by car to his office in Bath, valuing the time he had alone with his own thoughts driving through the peaceful countryside. When he recalled the dull routine of his daily commute in London, the sullen faces of the anonymous crowds packed intimately tight in the confines of the underground, and pavements of purposeful people driven like ants towards their goals, he was happy to have escaped. How ironic, he thought, that it was the sadness of his father's fatal illness that had so changed his life. The shock of the unexpected news had prompted his proposal to Belinda, and ultimately provided him now with such contentment.

Despite Jack's new role as Toby's godfather, he and Lucy continued the routines of their daily lives in London with little or no mention of children. For Jack children equated with moving, and the longer the subject could be ignored, the longer he could remain in the convenient bubble to which he had become comfortably accustomed. News of the American moon landing in late July generated huge excitement with live television coverage; pictures beamed down from the moon of Neil Armstrong and Buzz Aldrin walking on the moonscape. Lucy was so moved by Neil Armstrong's words: "one small step for man, one giant leap for mankind", she repeated them with moist eyed emotion. For those few days she feared the astronauts may be doomed to spend the rest of their lives on the moon unable to return, and when they splashed down her relief was palpable.

"I had a call from Belinda this morning." Lucy said casually preparing supper, pausing to see if she had caught Jack's attention from the newspaper.

"Oh yes. How are they?" He answered lowering the

paper.

"Fine, but she's fed up with being pregnant poor thing, she can't wait to deliver her package. She asked me if I would be a godmother, and naturally I said I would be delighted."

"Oh that's wonderful. Then we'll have one each." Jack laughed, raising the paper to read again, hoping to cap that conversation.

Lucy continued cooking in silent reflection, plonking the plates down on the small table when completed to illustrate her frustration. "We can't go on like this Jack."

"What do you mean by that?" He responded getting up to come to the table.

"We're drifting. Others of our age are getting on with their lives, starting families, moving to the countryside or whatever. Take Hugh and Belinda. Three years ago Hugh was sharing this flat with you. Now he's living in a beautiful home in the countryside, married with one child – soon to have another – and you are living in the same two by four space. We never talk about our future, starting a family or where we want to live. I know you – like all men - consider bonking as a thoroughly agreeable pastime bestowed on man by our creator as entertainment before the invention of television but – and this may come as a shock - it's also convenient for procreation."

"This may not be the most opportune time to raise the issue." Jack said smiling. "But don't you think that if all the families in the villages of Africa and India were supplied with electricity and televisions, it would give them an alternative entertainment to bonking, and so substantially reduce the problem of their escalating birth rates?"

"Oh Jack you're not taking me seriously." Lucy sighed in mild exasperation.

"I am taking you seriously, but I'd like to understand what's brought this on? This sudden vehemence, it's so unlike you."

Lucy calmed down. "I suppose it was my chat with Belinda and her telling me all about their lives down there, little Toby's first steps and the delight she gets from watching his personality developing. It got me thinking about us and made me realise that, as I said, we're drifting. We go from one working day to the next, dine out from time to time, or we see a film at the cinema, and spend the occasional weekend with our parents in the country. Jack it's getting boring. We're young and we should be planning our futures; starting a family before it's too late. It's great to be asked to be a godmother to Belinda's next child, but I want to have a child of my own."

Jack sat eating steadily, absorbing the undeniable truth of Lucy's summary of their lives; an unwelcome truth for him to swallow. But he could see from her eyes that the subject had brought her close to tears, and must be handled gently.

"Darling you're right, somehow the days melt into one another and one does not realise time's passing and think about these things. Let's not get despondent. The rental contract on this pad runs out in a few months, so let's start planning, let's think about what we want to do, where we want to live and then get on with doing it."

Lucy's spirits noticeably perked up. She had been anticipating a more vehement rejection of her analysis of their lives, or the gentle reassuring persuasion of a salesman not to rock the boat, stay the course; it would all be alright in the end.

"Let's decide categorically that we will not attempt to renew the rent contract." Lucy said emphatically to maintain momentum. "That will be a good start. We know we want to have a family sooner than later, so let's at least think about moving down to the country where we could find a small house conveniently near to our parents. I realise that we would both have to commute each day to London, but it's much better to bring up a family in the countryside, and we don't want to have to move twice. A suitable house in the country would also be very much more affordable."

"When you say a suitable house in the country darling, just to be clear, you're not imagining anything akin to Hugh's rambling manor house he inherited from his father are you?" Jack enquired rhetorically to lighten the mood.

"Well Jack Strange I must say I am disappointed. If you

cannot provide adequately for your wife and family like other men of your age, I regret to have to inform you that I'm going to have to consider my situation." Lucy replied with mock seriousness.

"Actually, coming to think about it, a large house could be a lot of fun." Jack fantasised. "With lots of rooms, I could chase you around the house until I caught you each time in a different bedroom." He chuckled mischievously.

"Well you had better get on with it while you still have the strength to run about the house," Lucy giggled, "to say nothing of the energy to do it when you catch me."

They sat chatting with increasing openness and animation until bed time, as if a blockage in communication between them was being removed, allowing pent up thoughts and unspoken concerns to be released like the constrained waters of a dammed stream. Instinctively Lucy did not rise to Jack's evasiveness on the subject of children, deciding to let fate take its course unhindered. Warm in the privacy of her thoughts as they made love that night, she prayed that the tender fervour of their passion would seed a new life inside her: she had stopped taking the pill.

That weekend they spent at The Nunnery. Having woken Jack up out of the cosy comfort of his lethargy, Lucy was determined to pursue the momentum, and she knew the best way to achieve that was to involve his mother; any possibility of their moving from London to live nearby and start a family was going to animate her encouragement. On previous visits Lucy had noted Phyllis casually dropping comments about their plans for a family, particularly since Jack had taken on the role of godfather. Now she could add that she would shortly be godmother to Hugh's second child, provoking subtle parental pressure for Jack and her to perform equally.

"Did Jack tell you Hugh and Belinda have asked me to be godmother to their second child due any minute?" Lucy asked Phyllis at supper that evening, emphasising the word second. "There must be something in the air in Wiltshire. They've only been down there a couple of years or so and haven't stopped breeding." She laughed.

Jack glanced across at Lucy smiling in recognition of her tactics. "Yes I was happy when Lucy told me. Now we will have one godchild each." He said.

"That's all very well dear." Phyllis responded immediately. "But when are you two going to start having children of your own? Of course your father and I are already grandparents, but we seldom see Emily's two unless we go to Paris, and one certainly has not been tempted to do that this year with all the civil unrest."

Jack looked at his father for sympathy. "There's no defence against the pressure of two females simultaneously," he sighed with feigned capitulation, "but the good news is that that's the primary reason why we've come down to see you this weekend. We've decided not to try to renew the rental on the flat or to move to another in London. We want to move out to the country, see if we can buy a house somewhere near here."

"I don't know what you're earning now young man," Harold said, "but what sort of price range of property would you be able to consider?"

"Frankly I don't know. That's one of the things we plan to do this weekend: have a chat with the Abbey National, The Halifax or whoever, and look around the estate agents to get an idea of suitable properties in this area."

"We want to start a family as soon as possible." Lucy continued, determined that aspect should not be lost in the issue of home buying. "Our idea is that we would both commute to London initially until such time as I became pregnant, but hopefully that would only be for a comparatively short time. With our joint incomes considered we could secure a better mortgage I suppose."

"Well that all sounds very exciting." Phyllis concluded. "I was beginning to resign myself to the probability that you would never get around to it."

The following morning Jack and Lucy went into Tunbridge Wells driving through the country lanes past brown fields freshly ploughed, and the muted hues of autumn's rust covering the woodland foliage. A chill was in the air, mist hung over the river in the valley, and dark clouds crowded pale blue patches of sky, brightened by an uncertain sun. This was the countryside they knew so well from childhood, the stomping grounds of bottle parties, and wooded arbours of hidden assignations. Animated by their new sense of purpose, they enjoyed each other's amorous recollections of times before and after they met, cautiously determining in the privacy of their minds what may be said and what better left untold. Initial conversations at the Abbey National orientated them on the extent of a mortgage they might achieve on Jack's annual salary, and a stroll along the estate agents' window displays in the High Street confirmed that they would need some parental help, if they were ever going to be able to buy a small house in the area. In need of consolation they carried on down to The Pantiles and walked along the arcade, stopping sporadically to peer through the windows of the antique shops. At The Duke of York pub, where years before they had habitually congregated on Saturday mornings confident of meeting friends, there was none. Surrounded by the smoke and babble of the new young crowd in the bar they felt uneasy, self aware, strangely out of place in a place they knew so well.

"What a difference a couple of years make." Jack commented. "Where is everyone? I feel as though I've been asleep and woken to find all I thought I knew was a dream."

"Jack, let's face it, in many ways we have been asleep.

This morning we've been idly looking at mortgages for a small house with the idea of starting a family at some time. But while we've been aimless our contemporaries have been getting on with their lives. They are not congregating in some sort of Saturday morning marriage market mêlée any more. They have already got their mortgages, their homes, and they're pushing kids in push chairs around supermarkets, doing the family shopping for the coming week."

"What a scene of family bliss you paint." Jack chortled. "It makes one really want to hump one's way to success and happiness."

"So no change there then." Lucy giggled. "Isn't that your life's philosophy anyway?" she added, smiling reassuringly.

"On a more serious note, now we have a clearer idea of what is entailed regarding a possible mortgage based on my salary, I'll have to talk with my parents to see if they are prepared to help. Obviously the clever thing to do is to approach mother first, we know she is all in favour of our finding a place in this area to start our breeding programme."

"Jack you make it sound as if we're going in for deep litter chickens." Lucy reproved. "I'm sorry to say I can't expect any help from my parents, I know they're having a tough time managing on dad's pension already."

"Of course I understand darling don't concern yourself about that. I'm sure mother will be happy to help, let's drink up and go and see."

By early spring the following year Jack and Lucy had made good progress. After weeks of searching - enthusiastically assisted by Phyllis – they had bought a small house with a small garden in a quiet country lane close to the village green in Leigh. Converted from two 19th century estate worker's cottages into one at some time previously, the property was in good shape, made fresh and their own by weekends of painting. Furniture and furnishings were second hand or family hand-me-downs; sparse and basic with the exception of Jack's prized radiogram. It was an encouraging start conveniently located

within easy reach of the main railway line to London for their daily commute; so far all was going to plan. But when the early dawns, warmth and long evenings of summer that had cushioned the novelty of their daily routine had faded through the damp days of autumn to the icy chill of winter, Lucy became disillusioned and depressed. Standing frozen on the frosty platform each morning and in the corridor of the overcrowded train for the hour long journey repeated in reverse each evening, the incitement of her aspirations for a family life in the country was festering by her inability to conceive. At the christening of Hugh and Belinda's baby girl named Carla, Lucy had lovingly cradled her baby goddaughter in her arms, secretly praying that one day soon she would cradle a child of her own. In a quiet moment she had confided in Belinda over her problem. She said how thrilled she had been initially to convince Jack to leave London and start a family, but try as they may it was not working, and the more they tried without success, the more frustrating it became.

"That's probably because you're trying too hard." Belinda suggested. "You're too pent up, stressed, not by your job – although standing for hours each day in the train commuting daily doesn't help – but by your frustration at failure. It's self defeating. You'll see – convince yourself truly you really don't care one way or the other, and you'll probably get pregnant. It's strange I know, but apparently it often happens that way."

Not entirely convinced of the logic of Belinda's advice but prepared to give it a try, Lucy decided first to reduce her stress in a way she recognised. One step would surely lead to the other which may then lead to success.

"I've decided to leave my job and look around here for something local." Lucy announced over breakfast the following weekend in a tone that left no room for discussion. "My idea of moving to the country was for us to start a family, but it's not working Jack. I'm stressed with the daily commute and tired at night. You can relax when we get home, but I have to start cooking dinner. Don't get me wrong - I'm not blaming you - but anyone who knows anything about these things will tell you that in these conditions I'm never going to get pregnant. Nobody can say it's not for want of trying, Lord knows we seem to do it every night."

"Wow that came out of the blue." Jack responded, surprised by the vehemence of Lucy's statement. "Have you already given in your notice? What sort of job do you think you can do down here?"

"No I haven't, but in a conversation I had with my boss some time ago, I mentioned our plans to start a family and the possibility of continuing to do translation work for them from home. He was keen on the idea, maybe because I would cost them less. Anyway my plan would be to get a half day job locally – in an antique shop or something like that – and also do freelance translation work at home. When I do get pregnant – if ever – I would have to give up my job in London anyway."

"That's true, but I hadn't envisaged that happening quite so soon."

"Maybe Jack that's because you would rather I didn't get pregnant. Frankly I think you'd rather keep things conveniently controlled as they are. Let's face it, if you had a choice, would you choose to have kids?"

"Darling let's not fight about this. You're becoming obsessed which does not help, and you're contradicting yourself. You've just said we seem to do it every night….."

"We do." Lucy interrupted emphatically.

"Well not quite – although I really don't keep a tally on

these things - but knowing you're not taking the pill, why would I risk it if I had no intention of starting a family?"

"Because you find me irresistible I suppose." Lucy answered smiling coquettishly to dispel any tension.

"Yes that must be it." Jack agreed absentmindedly. "Listen, it's not my department, and I must admit I'm rather uninformed about these things, but have you had a chat with your gynaecologist? Maybe just doing it, as you say, is not enough. Maybe our love making has to be a bit more targeted."

By their first anniversary in their new home, Lucy had a new job working five mornings a week with Charles Reynolds, a young antique dealer specialising in 18th century English furniture in The Pantiles, leaving her afternoons free to work at home. Less stressed but not pregnant, she had consulted her gynaecologist following Jack's suggestion, and been assured that he could find no reason for her inability to conceive, other than self defeating over anxiety at not conceiving as Belinda had said.

"Well what did he have to say?" Jack asked on his return home.

"He said I was fine as far as he could judge, but maybe you have a low or lazy sperm count." Lucy giggled. "He also said firmly that you should give up smoking."

"What! Damned cheek, there's nothing lazy about my sperm I can assure you. No seriously, what did he say?" Jack continued; ignoring the issue of his smoking.

"Keep a strict record of my monthly cycle. As fertility occurs for only a few hours in the cycle - and apparently this varies from woman to woman - I have to take my temperature daily at the same time to ascertain the most likely time I could conceive."

"There you are." Jack responded. "I said we may have to be more targeted, although based on the law of averages, one would have thought we would have hit the target at least once already, bearing in mind all the times we've done it during the last few years." He laughed.

Over the following months Jack and Lucy complied with all the advice they had been given without success. Pressured by Lucy and fear of the mounting medical evidence of the fatal effects of nicotine addiction, Jack even succeeded in giving up smoking. But a cheerless air of unfulfilled expectation shadowed their existence, as if waking from sleep in hope of recovery to find nothing had changed in the night. The effervescent young wife who had welcomed his homecoming each evening had lost her bubbles in the concentration of her obsession. Making love no longer held the relish of impromptu acts of mutual lust or the slow burning arousal of excitation. Calculation replaced spontaneity, routine devoid of passion, little more than a physical function defined by the singleness of its purpose. But for Lucy it was more elementary, more selfless;

she had failed the basic function of womanhood. She tried to divert her mind from the issue; to immerse herself in her job; to discover another subject to occupy her mind and so dispel the clouds of failure by the creation of success. She set herself to studying and learning the names of the 18th century period masters of furniture design; the styles; the veneers; the terminology and how to judge a reproduction: but the only reproduction she craved was her own.

When Lucy missed her monthly period she did not mention the matter to anyone. Such was her excitement, her joy and fear she dared not tell a soul. She longed to tell Jack, to involve him in her delight, let him know at last that all their efforts had not been in vain, but instinct advised her differently. She smothered her emotions with chatter of her job, appeasing Jack's concern she find other interest to occupy her mind. After years of bitter disappointment she felt vulnerable, as if she were carrying an invaluable object of such fragility it could be destroyed by the smallest misstep. She pleaded tiredness in place of intercourse, taking no risks until all was more certain.

Although Jack became aware of the change in Lucy's demeanour he chose not to risk questioning why. The months of his constant understanding and collaboration demonstrating his love and caring for her frustration had taken their toll. He had grown tired of the ever present shadow of her fixation, and the enforced routine of recent months suffocating the customary rhythm of their lives. He had always considered himself one of the fortunate few for enjoying his job, but his days in London had become something more: an escape into normality. Crossing the Haymarket he spotted an old friend he had not visited for some time in the company of a stylish young woman giving added incentive to meet.

"Susie." Jack called out to catch her attention, dodging through the oncoming traffic. "How are you? How's James? Business as usual" He chuckled giving her a knowing look. "I'm feeling a little guilty for not having passed by to pester him for work recently, but I'm happy to say we're rather busy."

"Hello Jack." Susie said in the sweetly demure manner that veiled her promiscuity. "All's well with me, and all's well between James and me too, if it's not just the soap." She laughed, and noting his darting glimpses at her companion. "This is my friend Anouk from France."

"Hello Anouk." Jack said catching the scent of an inebriating perfume surrounding her. "I'm sure you must hear this all the time, but the only other beautiful Anouk I have heard of is Anouk Aimée, from that agonizingly romantic film 'Un homme et une femme' a couple of years ago. I can still hear the theme music in my mind. Tell me, are you also working at Luxus Travel?"

A hint of a shy smile passed across her face. "No I am

just here for holiday." She replied haltingly.

"I hope it's a long holiday." Jack said sheepishly, suddenly self aware and unusually lost for words. "I love France. I have a married sister living in Paris."

"*Ah bon*. I live in Paris also."

"But not married I hope." Jack responded recovering his usual flippancy.

"No." She replied innocently unaware of the implied flirtation.

Susie groaned. "Don't pay any attention to him Anouk, he's full of it. Jack darling you never change and we love you for it. But sorry we have to go, I'll give your fond messages to James, but come by," she winked, "I know he'd like to catch up with you."

As they parted Jack turned to catch sight of Anouk and caught her briefly looking back his way. Was she looking for him or a taxi he wondered? For him he hoped. In the brief time standing by her side he had absorbed her mentally; she was Mediterranean in the same way Belinda appeared Mediterranean: slim, olive skinned, medium height, straight jet black hair cut to just above her shoulders, a slender face with high cheek bones, full lips and dark brown, almond shaped eyes. He noted too that she was chicly dressed for summer with shoes he approved, and smiled to himself at the thought: shoes are so important he had come to realise; the unsuspected ingredient for him in matters of ultimate compatibility. He struggled to analyse the curious immediate effect he felt on meeting her; she was already dominating his mind. This was not the superficial force of physical lust that had propelled him into infidelity in the past. No. Somehow this was more profound; as though an intuitive recognition had passed between them; a subliminal stirring of mutual need and understanding. She exuded a quiet sophistication, an inner serenity he found bewitching, disconcerting in the concealment of her thoughts. On the cusp of obsession he knew he must see her again.

Back in his office later he telephoned Susie, attempting to hide the true purpose of his call in the diffused content of friendly chatter. After expressing his pleasure in bumping into her by chance and lamenting their meeting had been so brief, he casually mentioned her friend; deliberately forgetting her name to disguise interest.

"How do you know your French friend? She seems very nice."

"Come off it Jack." Susie teased. "I saw your eyes, the way you were looking at her. You've probably already estimated her bra size." She laughed. "Actually we met a couple of years ago on the beach in Deauville strangely enough. I was there for a short break that summer, and she was working in rather a chic boutique tempting me to spend money I couldn't afford. I was alone so we spent time together in the evenings. The day

I left to come home we exchanged addresses - as one so often does with people one meets on holiday, thinking one would probably never hear from them again - but somehow we have kept in touch. When she called me to say she was planning to visit London I offered her to stay with me."

"Susie you do me an injustice. I was just going to say she seemed very nice, that's all. Of course I only met her for a couple of minutes, but I must admit I thought she had an inner stillness which I found strangely attractive."

"Jack." Susie said in a tone of commiseration, as if he had just divulged a secret flaw. "When were you ever attracted by – what did you say – inner stillness? It has always been the size and shape of the important visible bits on the outside that interested you."

"Guilty as charged your honour. But somehow that's what's rather fascinating about your friend Anouk. Not the visible bits on the outside – as you so eloquently put it – but what she conveys from the inside…..although I'm sure her visible bits are probably attractive too." He chuckled.

"I'm happy to hear that Jack. I was beginning to think you're losing your touch as an old married man. I suppose you're hoping I'll help you contact her?"

"Well I won't try to kid you Susie darling because I can see you know me well, but if you would, I really would like to try to see her again. Is she here long?"

"No only a couple of weeks or less I think. It would

be wrong of me to give you my home number so that you can try to contact her without asking her first. Jack, you understand I will have to tell her a little about you – not what an unrepentant womaniser you are – but at least that you're a married man. If she says I may, then I'll call you. Fair?"

"Very fair Susie. Thank you. I'll pass by to see you and James soon anyway."

On Friday morning Susie called Jack and gave him her home number. "I told Anouk plainly that you're a married man so my conscience is clear. She seemed quite keen to see you again too. I can't think why." She chuckled. "It must have been the inner stillness bit that grabbed her attention."

"You're mocking me Susie, but thank you. I'll try giving her a call next week."

"No Jack I'm not mocking you, I mean it seriously. You must surely be aware that your romantic boyish charm plus an interest in a girl's mind and thoughts - rather than just her body - could be irresistible for many insecure women."

"Is she insecure?"

"Well…..I gather things have not been going well with her boyfriend."

Over that weekend Jack tried to expel thoughts of Anouk that repeatedly entered his mind: images of her face, her smile, and the circumstances of their meeting. He maintained the light hearted manner of contrived unawareness he had adopted at the change in Lucy's demeanour, despite a constant urge to question why. Observing her at times unnoticed, he smiled inwardly at the warmth of the thought of how much he loved her as his wife and cherished her as his best friend. How fragile and vulnerable she now appeared. The past months had been a considerable strain and she had lost weight. He was happy she seemed happier; relieved that for weeks the issue of pregnancy had not been mentioned and the gloom of despondency at last appeared to have been shed.

Since moving back to the area of their parents a weekend routine had developed: Saturday lunch or tea with Jack's parents and Sunday roast with Lucy's. At home or at The Nunnery with Lucy, Jack was not at ease with his parents because he knew Lucy was not at ease with them. A hint of formality hung in the air; an atmosphere of guarded anticipation and undisclosed judgements being made. Though time and familiarity had softened the edges of his mother's opposition to Lucy, he was aware of the latent possessiveness and rivalry underlying her opinions; her mother-in-law's instinct expecting conformity with the standards of her beliefs; the injury of criticism implied but never said. Admonishments were couched in the first person plural as: "I think *we* should clean the silver." for example, when what she really wanted to say was "the silver needs cleaning." Maybe it's understandable that ageing parents might unconsciously betray resentment in their ageing, Jack pondered; envy for the lost vigour of their youth. Mothers might begrudge the fertile bloom of daughters and fathers their son's virility.

In contrast none of that could be said of Lucy's parents. Perhaps a lack of ambition restricting income produced the benefits of geniality instead. Lunch on Sunday was relaxed in the warmth of its informality, with Bernard's gin and tonics on arrival in the shade of the trees on the lawn as the weather permitted, or in the sitting room where he might play his beloved piano. Jack got on well with Bernard and he enjoyed his quiet sense of humour. Later Lucy would help Joan in the kitchen preparing the meal; a mother and daughter team in happy collaboration: roast beef and Yorkshire pudding, or pork with crackling and crispy roast potatoes, fresh garden peas and rich gravy. Last summer Lucy had spoken with eager anticipation of starting a family, but when the accumulated frustration of months of failure caused snappy irritation, the subject had been tactfully dropped. Now nothing was said, but in the familiar contentment of the home she had known since childhood, it was good to hear Lucy laughing again.

On Monday morning at the office Jack called the number of Susie's home she had given him. He called quite early concerned that Anouk may leave. It was not her own home, he rationalised, and logic indicated that being on holiday she would want to make maximum use of her time to explore. The first time he called there was no reply. He left it a minute and tried again: no reply. His mind started to buzz with negative anticipation. Let's face it Jack, he said to himself, this is justice; you shouldn't be calling her anyway. Determination came into play; the more one can't have something, the more one wants it, and Jack wanted it. Anxious that maybe Susie had made a mistake with the number he considered calling her to check. Intuition told him that was not a good idea. How could she make a mistake with her own telephone number? He reasoned. And if she had pulled a fast one and purposefully given him a wrong number, calling her to check would not help. He tried again.

"*Alo.*"

Jack's heart jumped at the sound of her voice; relief that he had made contact. His mind was racing but he tried to contain himself; give a carefree impression.

"Oh hello Anouk. Good morning. It's Jack. I tried calling you earlier but there was no reply."

"I was in the bathroom." Anouk said softly. "Susie told me you call me but I did not know what time. It is quite early *non*?"

Jack absorbed the softly accented tone of her voice. Why was it that when she said an ordinary word like 'bathroom' it sounded so much more intimate? He thought. "I'm sorry if I disturbed you. Would you like me to call back another time?"

"No it is OK. I am finished and dressed now."

Jack knew he could not sustain this stilted conversation on the telephone. He knew why he was calling her - and probably she knew why he was calling her - but only he could come clean. "Anouk I would like to see you again." He said calmly. "I know you're on holiday and will soon be going back to Paris. I don't want to think that the few minutes we met on the street will be the only time we meet. I want to see you again."

"Jacques you are a romantic." Anouk replied. "Susie told me all about you. I know you are married," she laughed gently, "but I like to see you again too."

A torrent of thoughts streamed through Jack's mind. Having said clearly (if not rather dramatically) that he must see her again, he could not appear indecisive. He had checked his diary first thing on arrival at the office, and happily there was nothing too pressing he had to do. He made up his mind to devote his time whenever possible to being with Anouk.

"Are you free for lunch today?" He asked.

"*Oui bien sûr.*"

"I know you're staying with Susie, but I don't know where Susie lives."

"Her apartment is in Hammersmith near the metro, so I can come to you."

"Hammersmith is on the Piccadilly line so it's very easy for you to come to me or for me to come to you."

"I do not know any restaurants here. I think it better I come to you."

"I could meet you in Knightsbridge – near Harrods. If you get out of the tube – the metro - at Knightsbridge, we could meet at the side door of Harrods. The street is called Hans Crescent."

"OK I will find it. What time we meet?"

"Half past twelve. Is that OK for you?"

"*Oui…..douze heure et demi. Bon.* I will be there."At the allotted time Jack approached their meeting point anxious that Anouk may have got lost on the underground. Would she be there? To ease his conscience at playing truant from the office and keep his mind off the excitement of meeting her again, he had visited a client in the area during the morning. He could see people standing at the door, but she was not one of them. He looked at his watch again. 12.30pm. He was always too punctual. With his back to the entrance he stood and watched left and right up the street; he would see her approaching; she should appear from the Underground Station entrance on the corner. Suddenly he felt a tap on his shoulder, a stab of nerves in his stomach. He whirled around.

"*Alo* Jacques." She said smiling and leaning forward to give him a peck on the cheek. "I am sorry. Did I shock you?"

Jack was flustered: he had not anticipated her arrival from behind, neither had he anticipated her kiss, and in the second it had taken him to turn, he had prayed fate had not sent a friend to ruin his liaison. "No it's wonderful to see you Anouk." He said laughing with relief. "I was not expecting you to come from behind that's all."

"After you telephone me this morning I had nothing to do in Hammersmith so I came early to look around Harrods. It is very nice but very big. I get lost." She laughed.

"There's a little Italian restaurant I know just around the corner. Is that alright for you? Do you like Italian food?"

Chatting over lunch they got to know each other, their first tentative phrases of polite conversation gradually evolving into animated mutual discovery as they found the comfort of confidence in each other's company. Jack spoke openly of the strange attraction; the draw towards her he had felt in the few minutes they had first met on the pavement, and was thrilled when she said she had felt the same. "You turned to look back." She said. "And you were looking back too." He laughed. He said he would like to see her as much as possible during her stay, and when she told him she was leaving on

Saturday at the end of that week, a tinge of panic swept over him; an impotence to prevent something dear being snatched away. Neither mentioned his marriage, as if ignoring the subject negated its reality and they could exist happily, if only for that time, in a self-indulgent world of their own. Each day that week they met. They went to street Markets; ate plump black cherries from the fruit stalls in Berwick Street; warm doughnuts in Spitalfields; and revelled in the antiques in Portobello Road. They went to The Tower of London; the Prospect of Whitby Pub overlooking the river; and on The Big Dipper at Battersea Fun Fair. They talked for carefree hours in coffee bars and restaurants immersed in the reflected joy of being together; they had fallen in love. On Friday afternoon Jack knew he must say goodbye. Over lunch he had become thoughtful, his conversation subdued, and the buoyant momentum of his spirit slowed under a cloud. They held hands across the table and spoke of seeing each other again; she said this was *au revoir* not goodbye. Anouk suggested he come back with her to Susie's house, but he knew that being alone with her would only prolong the agony of the inevitable and he refrained, despite the force of the temptation. He was obsessed and could not face the impending thought of losing her. At the peak of his turmoil and wanting her so badly, he feared the risk he might disappoint.

From Leicester Square Jack walked to Charing Cross and caught his train home. Anonymous in the crowded compartment his mind wandered through the bank of images and memories of his days that week with Anouk: the warmth of her smile; her laugh; the cadence of her voice; her bewildered expression at the cockney cries of the market stall holders. He sniffed his hand for a hint of her perfume. A lump rose in his throat and he fought to restrain his tears. Gazing out of the window as the suburbs flashed by, he recognised his weakness in having been attracted on sight to many young women; he had enjoyed a passionate, detached physical affair over months with Belinda, but the pain he now felt he had not felt since first meeting Lucy. How unfair of life, he said to himself, that one should have to suffer such agony for the beauty of romance; the reciprocal thrill of mutually declared love. Why had nature not provided in mankind an innate biological function to prevent such innocent suffering? How much more simple, less painful, less complicated life would be if we were born with some button to press, some switch to turn off at the altar.

As Jack drove home from the station in the soft evening sunlight he collected his thoughts, determined not to show any signs of emotion. He entered the hall but Lucy was not there with her usual welcome. There were no signs or sounds of life; only the resonant silence of solitude. He thought she must still be with her mother; he knew her father had not been well. A muffled sound alerted him coming from the sitting room and he entered slowly concerned as to what he may find. Huddled in an armchair like a child

Lucy was sobbing silently and a massive wave of panic

swept over him. How could she have found out? Who knew? Who would have told her? He had been so careful, so deliberate in keeping to his usual routine all week so as not to cause suspicion.

"Darling what's the matter he asked?" dropping on his knees by her side, fearful of her answer.

"I've lost it. I've lost our baby." She whispered.

In that moment of relief Jack thought his wife was hallucinating, that the pent up stress of her inability to conceive over so many months had temporally tipped her mind.

"What child? He asked gently.

"Oh Jack….." She said struggling to speak through her tears. "I have so longed to tell you for the past two months that maybe at last I was pregnant, but I dared not tell you or anybody until I was sure. Earlier this week the doctor confirmed my pregnancy. I was going to tell you the good news tonight so we could celebrate. But suddenly this afternoon I started to bleed heavily. I'm so sorry Jack," she said sobbing again, "I lost our baby."

Chapter 7

Assent To Temptation

Over the following weeks Jack was determinedly loving and supportive of Lucy, vainly trying to flush out the burden of guilt preying so heavily on his mind; the turmoil that, at the time of his juvenile self pity in the train she had been in such despair, bleeding her miscarriage at home alone. He tried to convince himself that if only Lucy had told him from the outset that she may have been pregnant, maybe then he would not have allowed himself the freedom of mind to become so attracted, so obsessed with Anouk. But he knew in his heart that was not true. He had been content to see Lucy happier because it had been convenient for him. For his own selfish interest he had not questioned why for fear of risking further despondency. Try as he may he could not turn the clock back; rub out from the record his attraction for Anouk, and the carefree time and affection he had shown her. He had met her, become obsessed by her and fallen in love; it was an illness only time could heal.

With the scent of autumn in the air, Jack suggested to Lucy they should get away for a few days before the onset of winter, go somewhere neither had been before. With their budget stretched on other priorities after buying their new home, they had not been away on holiday. He hoped distance and discovery might help to distract her mind, dissolve the heartache of her expectancy crushed by loss. Since her miscarriage he had made a point of getting home as early as possible, and sometimes in the evening sunlight they left the limited confines of their small home and garden, to walk hand in hand over the spacious village green. The warm summer days of cricket would soon be over; the chestnut trees bordering the road turning brown, and children grappling on the ground beneath to gather the shiny fallen conkers. Lucy suggested a return to Paris; it would be easy and convenient, but Jack was not keen, saying she had lived there and knew the place well. He wanted to visit a place they did not know, a place so full of history, art and beauty it would occupy their interest and enthusiasm, leaving no time or inclination to reflect on the incidents of their immediate pasts. They decided on Venice.

From the airport they took a water taxi skimming across the shallow lagoon, the semi silhouetted form of the city, sandwiched between the sea and the sky, appearing to float on the near horizon, illuminated by the oblique golden rays of the fading evening light on its domes and towers. They had barely landed and already they were silently enraptured by the novelty of their arrival and the beauty of the city, as the detail of its ancient structures steadily drew into sharper focus. In Jack's imaginings it was as if he was a knight on horse back galloping towards a mirage; a medieval walled city afloat on a plain. As they came to the outer walls of the buildings on the perimeter, the boat slowed to a walking pace and entered a narrow canal. Daylight had dimmed to dusk. Mouldering façades rising high on either side falsely betrayed their building's dereliction; the relative prosperity of the original occupants conveyed by the size of the windows, and the grandeur of raised entrances splashed by the lapping waters. Absorbed in muted wonderment, they gazed left and right up sombre canals lifeless in their gloom. The figure of a gondolier appeared like an apparition out of the darkness silently easing his way home; the subtle rhythm of his single oar rippling the reflected lights from lower windows on the blackened water. Unaware of their whereabouts in this unknown destination, they passed under little bridges and small boats pottering about their business, and then suddenly, like miners rescued from the bowels of the earth into the dazzle of daylight and joyful crowds, they emerged from the dreary backwaters into the illuminated bustle of the Grand Canal. At last a scene they could recognise.

"Oh look.....the Rialto Bridge." Jack exclaimed excitedly.

"Wow it's quite busy, so many boats large and small going up, down and across; this must be their rush hour." He laughed.

"It's so beautiful." Lucy said softly. "If you half close your eyes, one can imagine a Canaletto painting coming to life; the colourful bustle of how it would have been centuries ago. It's no wonder Hugh and Belinda so loved it here for their honeymoon."

They passed under the Rialto Bridge and headed towards the right hand bank of the canal. Their hotel, the Pensione Accademia in the area known as Dorsoduro, was perfectly located near the Grand Canal, and overlooking the San Trovaso Canal with its own jetty. In the darkness of their arrival it could not have been more convenient.

"Well that was easy." Jack said with relief putting down their suitcase in their cosy room. "I must say I was dreading the possibility of having to find our way through narrow alleys following a street plan in the dark." He looked up at Lucy standing in the middle of the room, absent, a wan look on her face, her mind in another place. He wrapped his arms around her gently kissing her forehead. "Darling," he said gently, "I think the best plan now is to have a quick wash and brush up, and then try to find a little restaurant nearby for tonight. We can't be too fussy, it's getting quite late and I'm sure you're tired after the journey. We can explore, get our orientation better in the daylight tomorrow."

Over breakfast on the garden terrace in the sunshine Lucy appeared more animated, more engaged after a good night's sleep. They studied the guides they had collected; there was so much to do, so many treasures to be seen, it soon became mind boggling. In the few days they had there, how could they do it all? There was a risk of exhaustion before they had started. There was clearly a lot of walking ahead. If they went from one 'must be seen' to another without a plan, they would waste a lot of time and energy. Jack suggested a strategy: the city centre was divided into five areas; they should decide what and which sights most interested them in each area, and tackle one area after another. Today they would take it slowly, concentrate on where they were: Dorsoduro.

Each morning they followed their plan, the pain of their aching legs dissolved in the wine assisted reminiscences of their day's events over dinner at night, in restaurants chosen as much for the attraction of their canal side locations, as the recommendations of their cuisine. They marvelled at the splendours in The Doge's Palace; the awesome magnificence contained in Saint Mark's Basilica; the beauty of Tiepolo's ceiling panels in the Scuola Grande dei Carmini; and Titian's altarpiece in the church of Santa Maria Gloriosa dei Frari. "It seems unjust," Lucy commented, "that one small city should contain so much treasure." They strolled through countless narrow winding alleys; the colourful fruit and vegetable morning market in Campo San Margherita; the hubbub of the Rialto fish market's bounteous offerings of weird creatures from the deep; along canal embankments, and up and over pedestrian bridges, alive to the centuries of history stored in the fabric of the buildings, and the grandeur of the palaces all about them. Resting in cafés over coffee or a glass of wine and delicious *Cicchetti* snacks for lunch, they watched with ironic amusement the distracted gapes of tourists pursuing their goals, and locals going about their business. Jack decided he had a soft spot for the Italians: he related to their inherent rebelliousness. He liked their joviality, their cocky self assurance and the self serving pragmatism they applied to their interpretation of the law. Out of the apparent disorder and confusion, somehow it all seemed to work. Too soon it was time to go home; they had seen a lot but there was so much more to be seen, and they vowed to return. Not once had they mentioned the shadow of home. They were happily together and made love again. Maybe Jack's plan had worked.

As the last vestiges of nature's autumn colours shrivelled into the stark silhouettes of winter, Joan suffered what was later diagnosed as a mild stroke. It was mid morning, and as she was making coffee in the kitchen with Bernard she felt vaguely dizzy, and a curious numbness on the left side of her face. She tried to speak to Bernard standing close by, but the words became incomprehensible in the contortions of her mouth, and the blank stare of numbed bewilderment on his face did not help her confidence. Unnerved by the strangeness of her physical inabilities and at a loss what to do, she complied with her intuitive reaction and went to lie down on her bed. Bernard telephoned Lucy at home anxious in his ineptitude, but there was no reply. He remembered then that she worked at the antique shop in the mornings so he called there, and a flood of relief passed over him when he heard her voice. In deliberative tones of panic contained, he tried to explain what had happened but Lucy cut him short. "Daddy," She said crisply. "Call doctor Humphries immediately…immediately. I'm coming now."

When Lucy arrived at the house a strange silence of emptiness pervaded. She had expected to hear voices; the doctor's voice to give her assurance, but there was none. She rushed up to her parents' bedroom dreading what she may find; the doctor had not as yet arrived, but happily her worst fear was also not realised. She stood by the bedside and took her mother's hand in hers to give her reassurance. Joan looked up at her daughter and tried to smile but it would not form on her face. A look of vulnerability in her eyes spoke of all that was going on in her mind. After the doctor's examination he confirmed Joan had suffered a mini stroke, and he prescribed various medications to treat her condition. He took Lucy aside and told her bluntly that this was a warning: the effects of too many cigarettes; too much alcohol; and the strain of too many daily household chores at her age coming home to roost. He said she had been extremely fortunate it had been so mild, but she was not out of the woods and that the next few days were critical; she must rest completely and undisturbed.

Over the following weeks Lucy did the household catering in the town when necessary before going to the shop in the morning, and each afternoon she came by to cook and prepare food for her father to heat up for lunch or dinner. She then went home to prepare dinner for Jack. "If I cannot conceive a child to take care of," she remarked bluntly to her father, "at least I can help take care of my mother." Gradually Joan's faculties recovered, but the experience left her apprehensive of any symptoms she felt or imagined. Bernard did the best he could with the daily help of Lucy. He did not play the piano for concern of disturbing Joan, and distracted himself pottering around the house being attentive to things not requiring attention. He worried if the worst should happen, and he was left alone, how could he cope? Over the many years of their marriage he had routinely dedicated himself to his work, while Joan had taken care not only of the shopping, cooking and other domestic requirements, but also the small practical demands of any household. Like so many men of his generation he had not learned the practical necessities of self dependency in his youth. In his mind he could hear Joan's voice telling Lucy in moments of exasperation: "He's incapable of changing a light bulb."

During the period of Joan's recovery Jack knew he must be patient. The short trip to Venice with Lucy a couple of months previously had proved a successful diversion for both - albeit for different reasons - and since their return she had retained the momentum with a positive attitude. She had her hands full with her work at the antique shop as well as all that was required taking care of her mother and father. Often when he returned home from London she had not yet come home and the house was in darkness. It was not something he begrudged; at moments such as these he was happy in his own company, and had fallen into a routine of a whiskey and soda and television. While they had been in Venice he had been so engrossed in the wealth of the city's treasures, Anouk had barely entered his thoughts. But since returning to the drudgery of his daily commute, memories of those few days they had together returned, needling his mind. Common sense and a small spark of conscience told him to resist the temptation to contact her again, let bygones be bygones, but he found it impossible to accept that theirs had been merely a transient relationship; 'ships that pass in the night'. When he had left her the last time their good byes had been so indefinite, he had no clear idea at all as to what he hoped to achieve, all he knew was that he had to see her again.

With Joan fully recovered and back on her feet again, Jack suggested to Lucy that she take a short break over the following weekend and pay Hugh and Belinda a visit. He explained that he was sorry that he would not be able to join her as he had to go to Stockport that Friday, and would not be back until Monday evening. He concocted a story that one of his most important clients, Green Shield Stamps, were making a large promotion in collaboration with Tesco who were opening a new supermarket, and he had to be there to ensure all went smoothly. Lucy was not suspicious; Jack had made trips around the country like this before.

When Jack telephoned Anouk she said she was surprised to hear from him after so many months, but the detached tone of her voice seemed to express little pleasure in the surprise. She appeared distant, uninvolved, and the warmth of the affection he had known was no longer present. To explain why he had not called before, Jack told her all that had taken place since they had parted. He said he had thought of her constantly and wanted so much to see her again. Anouk said she had got back together with her boyfriend Gilles. Jack asked if they were living together now, as that would negate the reason for his call, and was pleased when she said no. If she really wanted to put him off, he said to himself, she would have said yes. To keep matters simple, Jack said he was coming to Paris that weekend to visit his sister; he had his flight tickets and was arriving at

Orly on Friday night. It was not true, but his instinct was guiding. By saying he was coming to Paris anyway, seeing her was supplementary. If she thought he was coming to Paris only to see her, she may want to put him off. At the end of a stilted conversation they agreed: she would collect him off his flight at the airport.

As Jack emerged into the arrivals concourse Anouk was standing there, and in that moment he saw her as he first saw her when they had first met. It was as if time had stood still, and the same surge of attraction flooded through him; to sweep her up and make her entirely his own. As he approached, a mutual shyness seemed to hang between them. He put down his small suitcase and they embraced hesitantly.

"It's so wonderful to see you again Anouk." Jack said relishing the sensory recall of her perfume. "I've been dreaming of this moment."

"*Ah bon*. It's good to see you too Jacques." She said casually. "I must say I was thinking I would not hear from you again. But here you are." She laughed ironically. "My car is in the parking."

They walked in silence to the car, each engaged in the privacy of their thoughts.

"Wow - a green Volkswagon Beetle convertible." Jack said admiringly. "I would love to have one of these."

"Yes I love it too. Do you want me to drive you now to

your sister house?"

"No I don't think I can stay with my sister. She only has two bedrooms, he lied; she and Francois are in one and her two children in the other. I think I will have to find a hotel. Maybe you know a good, cheap hotel near you where I could stay?"

Anouk did not respond to that proposal, and for a while there was silence in the car as she drove in the dusk through the southern suburbs, across the city centre, and out again.

"Have you had something to eat *ce soir*?" Anouk asked.

"Yes I ate a couple of sandwiches at the airport while I was waiting for my flight."

"Are you hungry? I can make something easy for us when we get home."

Jack did not respond. Anouk had not said a word about a hotel since he had mentioned it, and he did not know whether having something easy to eat at home came before or after taking him to a hotel. In a perfect world, he said to himself, he would be staying with her, but so wishful was his thinking he didn't dare ask. They appeared to arrive at their destination when Anouk drove down a concrete ramp and entered a dimly lit, cavernous underground car parking area. She entered a numbered vacancy which Jack took to be her designated slot.

"Is this where you live?" Jack asked as they clambered

out of the car. A dull smell of petrol and the accumulated years of exhaust fumes layered onto the concrete fabric of the building hung in the cold, damp air.

"Yes I have my apartment on the tenth floor. We can take the lift."

"Aren't you concerned about coming home here alone at night?" Jack asked looking anxiously around him at the forest of columns and dark cavities that could conceal potential muggers.

"Of course I was at the beginning. But now I am used to it. I always have pepper spray in my handbag, so be careful." She chuckled.

On entering the apartment Jack could see straight through to the lights of Paris like an illuminated carpet lying out before him to the horizon. The scent of Anouk's perfume pervaded throughout in the air. Looking around, he could immediately relate to the compact accommodation; it reminded him of the roof top flat where he had lived in London: a small sitting / dining area with an open kitchen and narrow terrace, two bedrooms and one bathroom all functionally modern, restrained, ordered; absent of any florid elements of girlishness.

"Do you want to stay in a hotel Jacques or would you like to stay with me?" Anouk asked in a matter of fact tone.

"Why do you ask me like that Anouk? Of course I want to stay here with you, but I didn't want to presume I could stay with you when we spoke on the telephone. For some reason our conversation was difficult, it was strained, as though we didn't know each other well. All I knew was that I wanted desperately to see you again, but I had the impression you were not sure. Perhaps you're still not sure?" Anouk did not respond. "When we were together in London," Jack continued, "you were very affectionate, but now I have to notice that you are rather distant. You told me that you had got back again with your boy friend Gilles. I fully respect that, so if I am a problem for you, if you would prefer me to stay in a hotel, OK I will find a hotel. But if you are happy for me to stay here over these few days, I would love to be here with you."

"First we open a bottle of wine." Anouk said plonking a bottle of red, two glasses and a corkscrew on the kitchen counter, and looking meaningfully at him to open it. "I will make omelettes for us and we can talk. Talking is a little easier with a glass of wine, *n'est pas?*"

"By the way, what is the perfume you wear?" Jack asked as he opened the bottle and poured two glasses. "I noticed it the first time we met on the street in London."

"It's called Vetiver by Guerlain."

"It's intoxicating." Jack laughed. "Whatever lies ahead for us, it's a scent I will always associate with you."

Anouk looked up from the cooker sipping her wine. "You say whatever lies ahead for us Jacques, but you know in your heart there is nothing ahead for us, not together. You are a romantic but…..how you say in English…..*Ah oui*, you want your cake and eat it. You are married, and we both know you love your wife and will not leave her. And I do not want you to leave her."

"But you agreed to see me in London…..you knew then that I was married." Jack responded taken aback by the clarity of Anouk's words.

"*Bien sûr*. You were attracted to me and I was attracted to you. Yes I knew you were married, but I was on holiday……"

Jack interrupted. "So for you it was just a game, something fun to do in London on holiday."

Without responding Anouk came around from the kitchen counter and put two forks and plates with omelettes on the table. She sat down. "No Jacques. Please do not be a child." She said dryly. "When I said I meet you in London, I did not think we would fall in love…. yes Jacques I fell in love with you too, and it was very painful when you had to go. After I got back to Paris I thought about you night and day. I hoped you call me but you did not. Since then I have had a lot of time to think about it, and I am now very clear in my mind that I have to get on with my life. As I told you, Gilles and I have got back together again. As you can see we are not living together – we are taking things slowly – but maybe we will again in time. What I know is that I cannot live alone in hope that you will come to live with me and we will be happy for ever; like a romantic story."

They ate their omelettes in silence, self consciously sipping their wine periodically as a means of injecting some element of purpose into their mutual unease. Jack shuffled in his chair as a prelude to breaking the tension.

"So why did you agree for me to come over to see you this weekend?" He asked calmly. "You could have said all this on the telephone."

"Because you said you were coming over to see your sister. I understood from you that you already had the flight tickets, so I thought OK, if you are in Paris anyway, it may be better to speak with you directly."

Jack realised his plan had back fired. By pretending he was coming over to see his sister, and thereby giving the impression that seeing Anouk would be a very pleasant supplement, he was now left with no rational response. The only way forward was for him to accept the situation.

"Anouk I have to understand all that you say, and I really do not want to hurt you any more than maybe I have already. You're right, and I have to accept the frustration that sadly I cannot have my cake and eat it as you say. I really fell deeply in love with you – I am still in love with you – but you know I love my wife Lucy and I cannot and do not want to leave her. As it is now quite late, maybe I can stay with you here tonight, and tomorrow I will find a hotel."

"No Jacques." Anouk said gently. "Of course I knew that your plan was to see me not your sister. But I wanted to see you too. You say you are still in love with me – *peut être c'est vrai* – but I have talked myself out of that luxury as, sadly, I know it will not end happily. I would like you please to stay here with me this weekend. We will have a good time, like the good time we had in London, but let's try to make sure we don't fall in love again." She laughed.

A flood of relief passed through Jack's mind, the paradoxical relief that comes with the acceptance of the cessation of an aspiration, ultimately found unattainable. Although the logic of Anouk's analysis of their relationship was irrefutable and the disillusion uncomfortable, her words had exposed the futility of his romantic notions, and put an end to a problem: a problem of his own making.

"Thank you…..that's a nice idea." Jack responded. "No, you're right, of course you're right I know, but it just seems unjust in the scheme of things that one can fall so much in love – become so obsessed – and yet those emotions can only be judged as illicit. In my next life I hope I return as chief in an African tribe so that I can fall in love and have as many wives as I like." He chuckled noticeably more relaxed. "I have a good friend from my school days called Hugh. We shared a flat together in London for years before I got married. He was my best man at my wedding. He's very correct, adult and conservative. When we were younger and I was always painfully crazy about some girl or other, Hugh would give me fatherly advice. Oh.....I don't know," he sighed, "maybe one day I'll grow up."

Anouk laughed. "Do not grow up too much or you will be boring like most other men. It's wonderful to fall in love, but unfortunately if it is serious, you must be prepared to make a decision, and the decision is inevitably painful."

They finished the bottle of wine chatting with an unguarded ease that the strained emotions of only a short time before had not permitted. Now they could be friends with so much more to say. Despite the single minded intensity of their relationship, they had only known each other for a few days, although each might have thought differently. Jack spoke openly about Lucy's longing to have a baby, how failure had fed endeavour, and endeavour exposed failure. He told of the many months of despondency that had clouded their home life, and the cruel twist of her miscarriage. Anouk told of her on and off relationship with Gilles, the petty problems and frustrations that had arisen from their trial living together, and her fears of making a commitment ending in failure. She said she had suffered as a child when her parents had divorced; she would not want to inflict the pain on any child of her own. She then laughed defensively saying their conversation was becoming maudlin, and suggested they should better go to bed.

Alone in bed in the darkness of his room Jack imagined Anouk asleep in the adjoining room, but strangely he felt no lingering lust to be with her. His mind churned with all that had taken place since his arrival, what had been said, and the disillusion of her inarguable rationale removing the burden of being in love. He chuckled to himself when, in his mind's eye, he saw himself as a balloon wheezing out its dispirited air, punctured by the undeniable obstacle of applied logic. He thought of Lucy at home with Hugh and Belinda, and how much he loved her, and prayed that one day he could give her a child of her own. He imagined her vividly in the bed in the room where they had slept together, and recalled the time he had stood over her asleep in the early morning; her face snuffled into the blanket, the soft down on her temples and long blonde hair spread over the pillow. He twisted under the duvet suddenly restless, and in that moment all he wanted was to go home.

When Jack drew the curtains the next morning, the vitality of the night illuminated city stretching to the horizon had morphed into the cheerlessness of a bleak urban landscape, extending far into the distance smothered by dense cloud and drizzle. To the left he could just discern the rise of the Sacré Coeur and the Eiffel Tower beyond. He had woken early, lying in bed mulling over his life, making no move until her heard Anouk go into the bathroom. From the sound of cups and cutlery coming from the kitchen he guessed she was now dressed so he could go and shave.

"*Bon jour.*" She said cheerfully when he finally appeared. "Did you sleep well?"

"Yes thank you. I think the wine helped. How about you? Did you have a good night?"

"*Oui merci.* I took some time before I fell asleep..... to much thinking, but then it was OK. Now I really need coffee."

Over breakfast they talked about things they had not talked much about before: her job in public relations; his job; her family; his family; and what they could do on such an awful day. The dank view from the window was not encouraging. Neither was in the mood to visit museums or suchlike they agreed, and with no ulterior motive now to hide, Jack laughed at the irony that he was now worried they might meet his sister or Francois by chance; the situation would be very difficult to explain. He accepted Anouk's point that in a large city of several million inhabitants it was extremely unlikely they would be in the same place at the same time, but he insisted it was Murphy's Law: if something can go wrong, it will go wrong. "Murphy's Law?" Anouk asked looking baffled. "Yes," Jack explained, "if you really do not want to meet someone, Murphy's Law says the chances are that you are sure to bump into them." The best plan he suggested was for them to go to the cinema, so Anouk looked in yesterday's paper so see what was on in the original English version: Goodbye, Columbus or Love Story, there was little choice, and Love Story they agreed, was probably not suitable entertainment for them at the moment. By late morning the sky had brightened a little and the drizzle had stopped. They took the car and drove into the city, parking in a street close to where the film was showing in the Boulevard Saint Germain. They found a bistro for lunch, and later as they left the film in the cold, wet dusk of late afternoon, Anouk suggested they go back to her apartment. She said with a wry chuckle she didn't like cooking (which Jack already suspected from the limited facilities in her spotless kitchen) so he should not expect a deliciously French home-cooked meal. But if it was OK for him, they could buy wine, a baguette, cheese, ham, salami and stay warm at home that evening. Jack happily agreed.

Jack lay in bed that night mulling over the day's events: his conversations with Anouk and recalled observations of her mode of life that had subliminally entered his mind. Differences in so many aspects of their lives filtered into his realisation. As an attractive young French woman who had grown up in Paris nurtured by the city, Anouk was self assuredly adult, street wise, and independent with an acquired sophistication. In contrast, Lucy conveyed naturalness free of affectation, the open spirited vulnerability of an English girl raised in the countryside: beautiful, buoyant and unguardedly warm hearted. He too was a country man by nature, he reflected; it must have been a subconscious reaction to this difference that had so attracted him instantaneously to Anouk: the attraction of opposites; yin and yang, black and white.

As the deepening sensation of sleep submerged those thoughts in his mind, Jack heard the handle of his door move, and a narrow shaft of light sliced across the floor and was gone. He felt the presence of a figure in the room and a hint of Vetiver. The duvet shifted and Anouk slid into bed beside him, erotically warm in her nakedness. He yearned to put on the bedside light to relish every inch of her body he had pondered for so long in his imagination, but instinct told him to desist. Raising himself up on his elbow he kissed her deeply whispering a plea into the indistinct image of her face on the pillow. "Oh God I hope this is not just a dream." He cupped her small firm breasts suckling each in turn running his tongue around her erect nipples, and put his hand down into the moist invitation of her crutch. She opened her thighs, and as he mounted her she drew back her legs guiding the steady penetration of his erection into her.

The brightness of the light through the curtains on waking the next morning told Jack it was a fine day, and in that moment he feared all his memories of the night had been a fantasy. Cautiously he turned and smiled; Anouk was still there asleep by his side. He lay still on his back staring at the ceiling recalling the events of yesterday. What had been said of significance over supper? What may have influenced her mind the previous evening that had caused her to come to him? Maybe alone in bed some provocatively erotic aspect of the film had played on her mind impelling her, or changed her mind, and she wanted to attract him to remain with her. Unable to find an answer to those questions he settled on sex; a compelling human desire well known to him. Why waste energy trying to analyse the motivation, he said to himself, when he was so content with the outcome?

When Anouk woke she turned and smiled at him sleepily. She put her arm out inviting him to come close. As they lay kissing and stroking with their naked bodies touching, Jack pushed back the duvet so in the light of day he could absorb her lithe body and breast which in the darkness of night he had only felt but not seen. She could feel the hardness of his erection pressing insistently against her thigh. She raised herself up on the bed and knelt over him, lowering herself to envelope him into her, slowly pumping up and down with increasing frenzy until she gasped and fell spent over him. They lay in silence for a short time each ruminating on the night's events and how their relationship may now have been affected. Suddenly Anouk threw back the duvet and got out of bed, announcing in a cheery voice "I am now going to take a bath *chéri*. You can come too if you like." Jack did not answer. In the circumstances he could not think of a better idea, although one other possibility had instantly entered his mind. He stayed in bed listening to the bath water running; the sound had always comforted him. Late at night as a child unable to sleep, uneasy in the spooky darkness of his room at home, he had been assured by the muffled babble of water gushing as his father took a bath before bed. He thought about bathing together now with Anouk, and smiled at the ridiculousness of his shy concern; only minutes before they had been stark naked, locked together in an act of carnal gratification. He got out of bed and went naked, self aware to the bathroom; she was lying deep in the steaming water, her black hair only inches from the bubbly foam hiding her body beneath. Gingerly he eased himself into the foam, facing her with his back to the taps.

"*Bon*. What shall we do today? She asked with the casualness of the familiar, as though they were sitting clothed at breakfast, and the night's events and this moment of intimacy were figments of a fertile imagination. "I think it is good weather, we could go to the Marché aux Puces..... the flea market."

Looking at Anouk and imagining the form of her body hidden in the watery warmth, Jack could feel the risk of his arousal. "Yes that sounds like a good idea. I love antiques. I've always wanted to go to the flea market in Paris, but I've never had the opportunity." he said slightly flustered and hoping mundane conversation would keep more stimulating thoughts from his mind.

They lay chatting in the warm suds with the relaxed intimacy of a couple well known to each other. She washed his back, and as he washed hers his hands slipped around her to embrace her breasts. She slapped his arm playfully saying he must not be greedy, and got out of the bath, wrapping herself in a towelling dressing gown. "I need a coffee. I will get the breakfast." She said, as Jack sank silently back into the water.

There was a large Sunday crowd at the flea market brought out by the fine weather. Jack was amazed by the size of the market, an endless maze of narrow alleyways with stalls and small boutiques on either side, each an Aladdin's cave burgeoned with antiques and curiosities: furniture large and small of all styles and periods; silver; glass; jewellery and collectibles; ethnic artefacts; garden ornaments and architectural salvage: he had never experienced anything like it. He was energised and engrossed with so many objects, asking the prices and replacing the articles cautiously on hearing the answers, as if considering a decision. They progressed steadily deeper into the maze until they came to the heart of the market. There was a bustling café with tables and chairs, and a spellbinding pianist wailing nostalgic - though incomprehensible - *chansons*, adding to the burden of his accumulating elation. They found a table, ordered a bottle of wine, and as they sat listening, an overwhelming surge of uncontainable exhilaration arose in him filling the cup of his intoxication to spill in silent tears of hopelessness: he was in love with life, in love with Paris and in love with Anouk.

That evening they went out for a simple meal in a local bistro and chatted over the day's revelations. Jack spoke animatedly of their hours in the flea market recalling the frustration of items he had coveted but could not afford. Unspoken was the shadow of the inevitable they both knew but were trying to forget: tomorrow it would all be over.

Later that night, lying in bed after making love, Jack turned to speak, but Anouk put her hand gently over his mouth to stop him. She knew no talk of love, intimacy or passion would change their insoluble situation; words only seemed to enhance its futility. Early the next morning the bedside alarm clock dragged them into the day; neither had any appetite for breakfast, just a coffee. Few words were spoken as they drove to the airport, and on arrival Anouk did not attempt to park the car, but stopped directly in front of Departures, unable to endure the extended pain of a prolonged farewell. They kissed, and as Jack went to speak, she raised her hand over his mouth again to stop his words saying softly "No Jacques please." indicating in her voice that she already knew well all he wanted to say. As he watched her drive away with tears in his eyes and an agonizing lump in his throat, his mind flashed back recalling painful memories of his childhood: the stomach churning pain he had felt as a small boy at the inescapable inevitability of being driven back to boarding school by his mother at the start of each term, and the wretched heartache he had then suffered as he watched her drive away leaving him alone.

Chapter 8

Murphy's Law

Seven years after her initial stroke Joan suffered another stroke and died; she was only sixty eight years of age. In the months of her recuperation immediately following the first attack, and for the better part of that first year, she had been pressured to accept the doctor's advice regarding her excessive consumption of alcohol and cigarettes, through Lucy's daily restraints taking care of her. But as time went on and Lucy's vigilance diminished through concerns of her own, old habits returned. Despite her determination Lucy had been unable to conceive the baby she so desired, and suffered the despair of two further miscarriages. She struggled not to show envy whenever she noted the tell tale sign of the swelling belly of pregnancy in one of her friends, particularly when they may already have other children. Thoughts entered her mind that had never entered her mind before: how could it be just that they have two or more and I have none. In self defence she adopted an exuberant pleasure in their good fortune, as one might when a friend wins big on a lottery, finding solace in the disguise of resentment: why not me? At home with Jack her moods swung from the loving, gentle affection he had always known, through apathetic indifference to a snappy intolerance; aggravated by the death of her mother. There were times when Jack had grown concerned about her mental health. Too often she had referred to the futility of her life; how fate was against her; the joys of birth denied in favour of the cruel sadness of death. But with time a grudging acceptance of their state took hold; a submission to the inevitability that she would remain childless. Her years of fertility were coming to a close - "the cut-off age of forty"- as she starkly described it to Jack. They had talked endlessly about the possibility of adoption, but Jack was not a family man by nature. He only wanted a family because he loved Lucy and she wanted a family, but he knew in his heart any child in their home must be one of his seed; if he was to love and care for it as his own.

Jack had done well in his job over the years he had been there, pulling in new business and expanding the volume of work from existing clients. He got on well with Bill Harris - they made a good team - and in recognition of his contribution Bill had given him a partnership in the company. Annual increases in income had enabled him to upgrade his Mini to a much prized Mini Cooper, Lucy had a

Mini of her own, and the second hand sofa, arm chairs and other items of furniture with which they had first decorated their new home, had been replaced with antiques Lucy had acquired at trade prices. They were able to take annual foreign holidays, often to the South of France renting an apartment in Port Grimaud, and more recently to the Hotel Villamil in Paguera on the island of Majorca, following enthusiastic recommendations from Jack's parents. At times, friends invited to dinner would remark on their material lifestyle and freedom with barely concealed envy; friends with children who took it for granted that children were a natural outcome of marriage: unthinking in the superficiality of their own material ambition that Lucy would willingly exchange all for the blessing of a child.

In the late spring Jack suggested to Lucy that they should get away for a week - maybe to Cornwall - he needed a holiday, and as she had been over burdened with the responsibility of caring for her father in the months since Joan's funeral, a break away may help her to clear her mind he suggested. But Lucy dismissed the proposal out of hand as an irresponsible idea, impatiently demanding who would look after her father while they were away. Jack suggested Brenda who helped Lucy twice a week at home with cleaning and other domestic chores. He pointed out her reliability; her kindness; her cooking skills; her ability to drive and the advantage of Bernard knowing her well. Faced with the inarguable feasibility of the idea, Lucy's irritation subsided as her sense of indispensability calmed, and she warmed to the idea.

"OK then, but not Cornwall. Let's go back to Paris. We haven't been back since our honeymoon. But this time I want to stay over on the left bank – the Rive Gauche – in the area I came to know well during my time as an *au pair*. I know all the little streets over there between the Boulevard Saint Germain and the Seine, Place Saint Michel to the Gare d'Orsay. The area is full of antique shops and little bistros, and plenty of small hotels where we could stay."

"Are you sure you wouldn't prefer to try somewhere else we don't know?" Jack asked; reluctant to risk the provocation of old memories. After the last weekend he had spent with Anouk in Paris, mental images of their intimacy had plagued his mind for weeks. Over the six years or more since then he had not contacted her again, and gradually thoughts of her had faded from his mind.

"No.....if you're asking me, this time I want to go back to Paris." Lucy responded emphatically. "The last time you said we should take a short trip, I suggested we go back to Paris, but you are always against it for some strange reason, after all, we did have our first naughty foreign adventure there and our honeymoon. I want to revisit the old haunts from those carefree days of my youth, when the thought of getting pregnant was the very last thing I wanted." She said with a hollow laugh."

Sitting in the taxi fluidly threading its way through the late morning traffic into the heart of the city from the airport, Jack sat holding Lucy's hand resting on the seat, gazing out of the window in silent contemplation: a raft of random memories drifted through his mind confined in the privacy of thought. As they neared their destination, Lucy became animated drawing Jack's attention as they passed landmarks from her *au pair* days that still remained: cafés, bistros and other meeting places, or the sites of well remembered locations that used to be, but were no longer there. Jack's sister, Emily, had arranged for them to stay at The Hôtel des Marronniers in the Rue Jacob, a small hotel with a limited number of rooms in the centre of the area Lucy wanted to revisit. The entrance was set back from the street, and at the rear a lush garden patio offered a haven of secluded peace away from the city hubbub. Their room was simple in the indeterminate manner of French provincial décor, with dark wooden beams betraying the historical age of the building. When Jack looked concerned Lucy remarked philosophically "It's got a large cosy bed; clean carpet on the floor; thick curtains; an en suite bathroom and it looks out onto the garden: what more do you want Jack, we're only going to sleep in it?" Jack looked at Lucy with a cheeky smile. "Only going to sleep? He asked suggestively. "If that's the case I really don't know why I came." He chortled. "Listen, while we're on the subject of insatiable appetites, let's not forget we're in France and they eat early. We can unpack later. Let's find somewhere local now for lunch in a nearby brasserie."

Back at the hotel Jack telephoned Emily to confirm their arrival and dinner with them at home that evening. Emily said that Francois could come by to pick them up by car, but Jack said it's so easy on the Metro, reminding her that they had done it before all those years ago on their first visit to Paris together; their naughty weekend as Lucy called it. Later as they strolled around the area, a pale sun was shining in a limpid blue sky urging the city into summer; the plane trees and chestnuts already in leaf along the wide boulevards. Jack was keen to stop every few minutes to look into the windows of the antique shops as they passed, but Lucy kept pressing him on, eager to show him where she had lived as an *au pair* on the third floor of a building on the Quai Anatole France, overlooking the River Seine. She said she had kept in touch with the family for years after she left Paris, but then with time their communications fizzled out as they inevitably tend to do. "Strange to think those little kids are adults now." She mused. "Maybe they're married with children of their own." At the front entrance she read the name plates of the occupants on each floor of the building with conflicting thoughts: did she hope the family still lived there or not? And if they did still live there, did she have the courage to ring the bell after all these years with all that that may entail? Maybe it's best to let it go; Jack's body language on the pavement clearly indicated his fear of getting involved; after all they had just arrived. But the question was answered for her; there was no plate with the name Meunier she recalled. They walked on and on in a huge circle, passed the house where Lucy had her digs during the months she was studying cookery at the *Le Cordon Blue,* returning on the Boulevard St. Germain. At Les Deux Magots they stopped; their aching legs yearning for the promise of rest offered by a vacant table and the irresistible temptation of the tray of cakes. They ordered tea for two; a chocolate torte for Lucy and a mill-feuille for Jack.

"I could sit here all day people watching." Jack commented. "The theatre of characters passing by is pure entertainment: croissant, baguette, butter, jam and coffee for breakfast while mulling through the newspapers, an aperitif before a light lunch at midday, and tea and cakes in the afternoon." He paused in feigned thought. "Yes, maybe somewhere else for dinner though." He chuckled. "Actually I've always liked the idea of being one of those philosophers sitting at a table endlessly engaged in existential debate."

"From what you describe of your daily routine, it sounds to me that you'd be a rather fat philosopher." Lucy giggled. "At what time are we expected at Emily's?"

"Seven."

"I think we should get back to the hotel soon. I need to shower and change. One always feels so grubby after a flight."

The musty smell in the stairwell as they entered the building was the same smell Jack had recalled the last time he and Lucy had visited his sister and family twelve years or so before. If any communal redecoration had taken place at some time, the old established odour had regained its hold. "If you blindfolded me and asked me where I was I would instantly know I was here." Jack said to Lucy as they climbed the stairs. In the intervening years since their last visit, they had seen Emily quite regularly when she brought the kids over to England to visit their grandparents. More often than not Francois had found an excuse to stay in Paris.

"Hello." Emily said in joyful welcome as she answered the door, embracing Lucy with affection and being lovingly enwrapped in turn by her brother. "It's so good to see you again; and here in Paris as well. It's been too long *mon cher frère*" she said in mock chastisement to Jack.

At the sound of their arrival Jules and Isabelle appeared smiling, with the awkward hesitancy customary to their teenage years, caught in the no man's land between child and adult; as if aware of the inevitable unspoken observations of their visitors' thoughts. They surrendered themselves languidly to the traditional kisses, and backed away content that they had been polite and performed their duty as they had been taught.

"*Bien venue.*" Francois exclaimed cheerfully, emerging from the bedroom in a scented rush of aftershave. "*Excusez moi* but I was late leaving the office and I had to have a quick shower and shave in your honour. Lucy you look wonderful as always." He said sweeping her up in his arms. "And Jack *mon brave*.....I don't know what you're taking, but you never seem to change a day."

In the sitting room Francois opened a bottle of champagne he had prepared and placed in an ice bucket, and after toasting each other, the conversation settled down to animated chat about the this and that in their respective lives since the last time they had met. Jack noted that Francois had aged in the intervening years, the leanness of youth had given way to a fuller form, and his black hair was noticeably greying at the temples. He had seen Jules only a year or so ago in England, but he was taller now, ganglier, and the smooth facial features of his early teens were roughened with adolescent pimples and spots; a blur of soft dark hair above his upper lip. Jack asked him about school, with anecdotes of his own academic failure; stressing the importance of qualifications to secure a good job. "Listen to your uncle." Francois said firmly to his son, as though Jack's words carried an authority: the added value of an independent source outside the immediate family. Jules said that he would sit his baccalaureate exams in eighteen months; if possible he would like to study media communication with a view to television journalism; he would have to do his one year compulsory military service some time, but was unsure whether he should do that before or after university. Lucy and Emily were engaged in women's talk, the occasional word caught on the air told Jack what that might all be about. Isabelle sat purposefully close to her mother on the sofa, as if to derive security from the combined vulnerabilities of their gender. She was in her mid teens now with long fair hair, blue eyes and a sylph like figure betraying pert breasts barely discernible under her floral blouse. Jack tried to imagine a father's thoughts with a daughter of that age, a reality he realised he would never know: how would he cope if she was his, aware that the childish innocence now conveyed in her pretty face, would soon be awakened by a hormonal onslaught, and adolescent aspirations for a woman's decorative trappings.

"Oh by the way Jack," Emily suddenly said over dinner in a conspiratorial tone of caution, "there must be a Jack look-alike out there on the streets of Paris."

"What are you talking about?" Jack asked chuckling. "What a very strange thing to say out of the blue."

"Yes you're right, but I've just remembered. A few years ago Francois came home and mentioned that he thought he had seen you on the Boulevard St. Germain. This guy was with a young woman with black hair. I remember Francois saying he only noticed, because the man had fair hair and the woman jet black hair."

As everybody started to tease Jack light heartedly he remained composed, entering into the sprit of the mock accusation, and looking directly at Lucy. He did not attempt to deny the story for concern that denial may only add weight to its authenticity.

"Oh if only it were true." Jack sighed with contrived longing. "I've always had this fantasy of having two women: one blonde and one brunette. I'm sorry if I've ruined any conspiracy theories - I do like the lunacy of conspiracy theories – but no, it certainly wasn't me. Actually many men have long hair too these days; it could equally have been two men."

"Yes that's true." Francois agreed. "In the student areas of St. Germain there are still some who haven't been informed yet that the hippy days are *passé.*"

"I haven't been in Paris since our honeymoon," Jack continued, "but it's good to know of another me roaming the streets. If I ever get into trouble here I can blame it on the other guy. You know, only the other day in London, I crossed Bond Street to speak with a man I thought I knew well who was looking in the window of Agnew's art gallery. I was so certain I put my hand on his shoulder and said "Hello Charles", but when he turned around, it wasn't the person I thought it was at all. I felt such an idiot." He laughed. "Oh yes….and I have another funny story too on this subject I must tell you. You kids will love this." He said chuckling at the memory. "A few weeks ago I was driving behind a car and there appeared to be a gorgeous blonde sitting in the passenger seat. Unable to resist taking a look I drew out to overtake, and as I was driving alongside, I took a quick glance to my right, but there was no gorgeous blonde: it was an Afghan hound sitting perfectly upright in the passenger seat."

Jules and Isabelle burst out laughing.

"You shouldn't be chasing blondes Jack when you already have a gorgeous blonde at home." Emily said. "Look what happens….you end up with a dog." She laughed.

"No I have to accept that you may have a point there my darling sister. But Lucy knows I only talk openly of my appreciation of blondes, precisely because I do have my very own gorgeous blonde at home." Jack said with sincerity smiling at Lucy.

It was not late when Jack and Lucy left. They had made arrangements to meet Emily for lunch in town the next day; it was Saturday, Francois would not be working, Jules had arranged to play football, and Emily was keen to spend the day at a friend's house. In the Metro Jack prayed Lucy would not return to the subject of Emily's curious story of his Parisian look-alike. Fortunately no mention had been made as a reference of how many years past this sighting had occurred, so hopefully any residual concern she may have, would be lost in the morass of insignificant events of time. The roar of the train in the tunnel discouraged conversation, and so much conversation had already been had that evening. Lucy looked at him and smiled, taking his hand and squeezing it reassuringly as if she could read his thoughts, and a pulse of guilt laden adrenalin shot through his guts. He thought how much he loved her; she was his soul mate, his best friend. Through their years together they had grown entwined like two inter supporting vines combine their strengths to support their vulnerabilities. He would be lost without her, and he could not bear the thought of her being needlessly hurt more, after all the pain and suffering she had endured.

Back in their room in the hotel Jack purposefully kept off any mention of their evening with his sister's family. Standing in front of the mirror in the bathroom washing his teeth, he caught sight of the reflection of Lucy as she undressed by the bedside; a daily routine he had known for fifteen years. As she stood naked, momentarily puzzled as to where she had put her nightdress and unaware of being observed, he saw her again as he had seen her on their naughty weekend: her figure still slim with her long blonde hair falling over her shoulders, her breasts full and firm. He thought how his sister's once youthful body had been changed over the years; she had a fuller figure now, and the firm nubile breasts he had once excitedly spied upon whenever possible when he was a boy of twelve, had been depleted into sad sacks by the eager suckling of babies. A mischievous thought entered his mind: yes it was tragic that fate had denied her a child of her own, but then every cloud has a silver lining. Tucked up in bed he reached out for her and she giggled, just as she had giggled all those years before. "Why sir," she said in mock surprise, "this is all so sudden."

The following morning after breakfast Jack said he wanted to take a walk around the area, look in the antique shops and find a book shop nearby called Shakespeare & Co., which Bill Harris had said was a must he should visit. Bill couldn't find the address at the time, but recalled it being in a tiny square by the river, near Place St. Michel, opposite Nôtre Dame. Lucy said she preferred to stay at the hotel for a while; the sun was shining, and she would like to read the paper quietly over coffee out in the garden patio before changing to go out for lunch. Following Bill's directions Jack soon found the book shop, and as he was browsing in the window before entering what he could see to be a rabbits' warren with books on shelves crowded up to the ceiling, he heard a voice calling "Non Jacqueline." A voice he remembered well. Instantly he turned to look and saw the back of a woman with jet black hair sitting on a nearby bench and a little girl close by; intrigued by the pigeons scavenging for crumbs from tourists' snacks. Casually Jack wandered around to get a view of the woman from the front, keeping his distance so as not to be noticed. There was no doubt in his mind it was Anouk. At first he thought he should leave, let bygones be bygones, but the urge to speak with her again was too great.

"What did I once tell you about Murphy's Law?" He said gently as he approached.

Anouk instantly looked up in astonishment. "Jacques. It has been a long time." She said in a measured tone, as if their parting had been only months before. "What are you doing in Paris?"

"I'm here with Lucy visiting my sister Emily."

"Is your wife in the bookshop?" She said with concern.

"No, don't worry, she stayed in the hotel. It's near here in Rue Jacob." He replied turning towards the little girl. "Is this your daughter?"

"*Oui*. Her name is Jacqueline."

"Yes I know; I heard you calling her. I instantly recognised your voice. That's what drew my attention."

"I had to stop her picking up the dirty pieces on the floor the pigeons are eating."

Jacqueline climbed up onto the bench clinging close to her mother; eyeing Jack with suspicion. "*Maman*." She asked. "Who is this man?"

"He is an old friend of mummy's *chérie* from England."

"She's very sweet. How old is she?" Jack asked.

Anouk hesitated, thinking before answering the simple question. "*Seis ans.*"

"Are you still with Gilles?"

"Yes we have lived together for years, but we are not married. Have you got children now?"

"No. No such luck I'm afraid to say. Poor Lucy has suffered a number of miscarriages. She got very depressed, but I think she's accepted now that for some reason or other, she's not destined to have children. She'll be forty next month so it's all a bit late now. By the way, I've never asked you. What does Gilles do for a living?"

"He writes books - *auteur* – and freelance journalist."

As Anouk spoke, an extraordinary thought prompted by intuition gradually percolated into Jack's mind, a thought he struggled to expel, but could not defy its insistence. No it cannot be, it mustn't be, he said to himself. He tried to remain calm. "You never showed me a photo of Gilles." He said casually. "Has he got fair hair and blue eyes like little Jacqueline?"

Anouk knew instantly where Jack's thoughts were leading. "Jacques we cannot talk now please." She looked around anxiously. "Gilles is meeting me here soon. He likes to come here to this book shop. I promise I will explain all to you, but I cannot now. Will you still be in Paris on Monday?"

The realisation that Anouk had read his thoughts and made no attempt to evade the situation or deny his fear of what he must assume to be the truth, left Jack astounded by the coolness of her attitude. Some extraordinary twist of fate had brought them to meet again in this place at this time, and he needed to know now. He could not wait until Monday; agitated in his desperation. He glanced at Jacqueline and smiled, as though confirmation of the truth was revealed in the actuality of her being. A look of dismay hung frozen on the little girl's face clinging to her mother's side, instinctively sensing tension, and Jack knew he must stop any thought of stubborn insistence; tears would soon draw inconvenient attention. Momentarily he felt giddy from the turmoil churning in his mind, the driving urgency for the truth to be released. "Yes." He replied bluntly.

"Then please try to meet me if you can at Les Deux Magots at 11.0 o'clock on Monday morning, you know where it is. Gilles will be working and Jacqueline in school. Don't sit outside where you can be seen; go inside to the back. I promise I will tell you everything. If you cannot come, please call me. I am living in the same apartment you know. Do you still have my number, it has not changed?"

"Yes it's still in my wallet."

"OK Jack. Now please go. I don't want Gilles seeing you here and asking a lot of questions."

Jack left them and wandered back towards the hotel.

He knew he must not hurry. He needed time to digest the extraordinary circumstance that had just taken place and to be himself before returning to Lucy.

"I'm back." He announced cheerfully, emerging into the garden patio and finding

Lucy ensconced in the pages of Le Monde. "It must be rather satisfying as an English person genuinely to be able to read a French newspaper. I must say I rather envy you that ability. I think if I was able to do that, I would ensure that I appeared as an arch typical Englishman, and sit conspicuously in a pavement café reading a French newspaper; just to impress others." He laughed.

"Well I've been doing that all morning since you left." Lucy sighed in feigned frustration. "And I'm really rather peeved nobody's come by to impress."

"Well I'm impressed for what it's worth." Jack said comfortingly. "Did you read anything interesting?"

"Not really. Of course the French are very interested in our General Election early next month; there's a lot of excitement about the possibility of Britain having its first female Prime Minister with Margaret Thatcher. By the way, what's the time? I left my watch in the room and couldn't be bothered to go and get it."

"Three minutes past eleven to be precise."

"At what time are we meeting Emily and Francois?"

"We said twelve thirty on the steps of La Madeleine.

They know a good brasserie in the area apparently. I could do with a coffee. Do you want another before we set off?"

It was a fine day so Jack suggested they shouldn't take the Metro or a taxi; they had time, and a walk would do them good. Walking together he had contrived, would provide diversions along the way, help maintain his natural composure and avoid any observation risking questioning as to what was on his mind. He knew he needed to mull back seven years through his mental calendar of time, check the sequence of events up to the present, and make an essential calculation: the year and month he had then been with Anouk in Paris, and the nine month period of a pregnancy plus the child's age. In his search for a rationale, a flash of irrational optimism entered his mind that maybe - just maybe - she might have taken another fair haired, blue eyed replacement lover in her melancholy after their separation. But instantly recognizing the naivety of the thought, he dismissed it from his mind. They strolled down through the streets to the Seine, over the

Pont Royal, through the Tuilerie Gardens and across the Rue Rivoli, suddenly finding themselves in the Rue Cambon outside the entrance to The Family Hotel; scene of their naughty weekend as well as their honeymoon. They lingered for a minute outside the entrance contemplating whether to enter for old time's sake but they did not; allowing those memories to rest undisturbed.

"*Bon jour*" Francois said cheerfully as they approached hand in hand, "it's wonderful to see you young lovers in Paris in the spring, how romantic." He laughed.

"Have you walked all the way?" Emily asked coming forward to embrace them.

"*Bon jour* and yes we have." Jack replied. "I hope you're suitably impressed. By the way, thank you again for dinner last evening, it was fun."

"Yes thank you." Lucy echoed. "It was fun and now we know Jack has a double." She laughed.

"*Bon* let's go and have some lunch." Francois said leading the way.

"What have you been up to this morning?" Emily asked.

"Well I've been lounging about reading the paper and drinking coffee in the hotel's garden patio." Lucy answered.

"And I went to find the Shakespeare & Co. book shop." Jack continued. "It's an Aladdin's cave for book lovers as you, of course, must know. I didn't stay long I must admit. To be frank, I think I was just completely overwhelmed."

After a short walk they entered a large brasserie bustling with the lunchtime trade of locals and tourists. The warm greeting the Maître d' gave to Francois and Emily clearly showed they were well known; their table reserved. They talked animatedly about their respective lives; some aspects of subjects they could not talk openly about in front of the children the previous evening. And later when Lucy left the table to "Powder her nose" (as she put it), Jack quickly asked Emily please to take Lucy shopping on Monday morning; just the two of them. He explained he really wanted to have the morning free to himself. Nothing illicit he assured them with a chuckle, only that he wanted to find a suitable present for Lucy's upcoming fortieth birthday the next month, and a morning of concentrated girlie shopping would also be good for her. Before they parted Emily made the suggestion to Lucy and she happily agreed, glancing at Jack for his approval.

"What will you do? Will you be alright on your own for a few hours?" She asked.

"Well I'll probably just sit around at the hotel, drink coffee and sulk."

"We could meet at Galeries Lafayette and take it from there." Emily suggested. "Let's say the corner entrance on Rue Lafayette at ten thirty; there's a Metro station there. Is that a good time for you?"

"It sounds pleasantly civilized to me." Lucy answered. "I look forward to seeing you then. Have a good day tomorrow."

Jack got to Les Deux Magots a little early on Monday morning. After breakfast in the garden patio of the hotel, he walked with Lucy to the Metro station at Place St. Michel, and after kissing her goodbye and requesting that she please not spend too much money, he bought an English newspaper in a kiosk before strolling back to the café. He took a seat on the banquette at a table inside at the rear and ordered a coffee. His intention had been to kill the time until Anouk arrived reading the paper, but nerves ensured he could not settle. He checked his watch repeatedly; read and re-read paragraphs numerous times without absorbing their context; continuously looking up as any movement caught his eye that could signal her arrival. When his watch informed him Anouk was a quarter of an hour late, nagging pessimism inched its way into his spirit: I knew it he mumbled to himself, I should have insisted on her telling me all while she was there in front of me; why did I trust that she would come when she must have known I would not pursue her? But then the thought occurred to him that maybe she wasn't coming because she didn't know. In the long hours of yesterday, reflecting on the bizarre event of his improbable meeting with Anouk, the thought had entered his mind that the whole episode may have been a figment of his imagination: a dream. After all, what were the chances of such an extraordinary occurrence happening in real life? And similar episodes had happened to him before: the confusion of dreams recalled with such clarity they appeared real. Maybe that night after supper with Emily, he reflected, elements in his subconscious mind at sleep could have tangled thoughts and images together as one: Francois's story of seeing him with a black haired young woman; recalled visions of being with Anouk; the innocence of Isabelle's young face; Lucy and the absence of a child in their lives. But just as he was about to give up, pay the bill and leave, he spotted a female figure standing silhouetted in the doorway, looking around, searching in the lesser light of the interior. The figure came forward into the room and Jack's spirits rose, it was Anouk; she had not failed him.

"*Bon jour.*" Jack said amiably, rising to greet her.

"*Bon jour* Jacques." She responded breathlessly. "I am very sorry I am late, but I had to wait a long time for the Metro this morning.

The waiter came by and they ordered two coffees. Jack tried hard to conceal his inner tension, but after waiting two days carrying and disguising this mental burden, he was impatient to get to the truth.

"Anouk." He said looking straight into her eyes. "It would be wonderful to be here alone with you as we were years ago, but clearly our circumstances have changed. As you live on the opposite side of the city, it was extraordinary that I should find you sitting on a bench in this part of Paris with your daughter close by. Fate must have planned for us to meet. I must say I don't really believe these things, but on this occasion it is very difficult for me to provide any other answer. After meeting Jacqueline, you know I know she is my daughter, so please I beg you, just tell me now the truth."

"Yes Jacques you are right; she is your daughter. That is why I named her Jacqueline." She answered simply.

Jack was surprised at the simple, unelaborated honesty of her reply. "Why did you not tell me?" he asked accusingly.

"Jacques." She said in an appeasing tone. "What good would it have done for you or me if I had told you? Immediately you would have thought that I wanted to pressure you in one way or another; for you to leave your wife, or to pay me money to support the child. I knew you would never leave Lucy – you love her too much – and I did not want to stain the brief, loving relationship we enjoyed by giving you the opportunity to think badly of me; that I had been irresponsible; got pregnant by mistake."

"What do you mean? Are you telling me it wasn't a mistake?"

"Yes Jacques I am, it was not a mistake. If you remember I came to you the first night we made love. I stayed with you to make love again the next morning, and we made love again that night. I was deeply in love with you, but I had to protect my own vulnerabilities. I had to accept that you would never leave Lucy, and in many ways I did not want you to risk leaving her as our relationship was certainly not secure. To put it simply Jacques: if I could not have you, I wanted your child."

"Would you ever have told me?" He asked weakly.

"No. Because I did not want to happen what has now happened. You are confused, you think you should have some responsibility, but you do not know what or how. You know that Lucy must never know; you have no children between you, so you now have a burden you must bear in silence."

"Will you ever tell Jacqueline who is her real father?"

"No, if possible I will not. She accepts Gilles as her father and they have a very good relationship. He loves her above everything - including me - and I beg you now that you know the truth, do not try to interfere in our lives. Think hard Jacques: you have nothing to gain and so much to lose; all you would achieve is heartache for everyone."

"Does Gilles know the child is not his?"

"It is a subject we have never talked about. Maybe he instinctively suspects, but he knows that too many questions often lead to unhappiness. Some things are very much better left unsaid. I came to you today as I promised to tell you the truth, and I have done that. Before I go now, I must ask you please to promise me faithfully that you will never ever try to contact me again or Jacqueline. Will you promise me Jacques?"

Jack was silent, his mind struggling to put into some rational proportion the magnitude of the outcome of what he had just been told, expressed with such simple honesty. A child of his seed had been born into this world:

a beautiful little girl with blonde hair and blue eyes that one day would become a beautiful woman, would get married, have children and grandchildren of her own, and die one day in some distant year unaware of her true origins.

"Jacques." Anouk insisted. "Promise me."

"Yes. It's hard, very hard, but you're right in what you say. Thank you for coming here to tell me everything, thank you for being so honourable, and thank you for your simple honesty. Yes I promise."

Anouk looked tenderly at Jack. She put her hands across the table and held his momentarily as she had done all those years ago in London on the day they first parted. "You're a good man Jack." She said rising to leave. "We must not allow ourselves to get emotional. This time sadly it is not *au revoir*, it must be goodbye." She came around the table and kissed him lightly on both cheeks, turned and walked away.

As Jack watched her passing through the door and disappear out into the street, he felt a leaden weight on his chest and the constricted ache of his tautened throat. He gasped and swallowed hard to fight back his emotions. Saying goodbye to Anouk each time they parted had left him drained, and this time it was so much more significant: he had promised never to contact her again and a daughter he had only briefly met and would never know. The waiter returned, as though through years of watchful experience of clandestine *rendez-vous* he had learned to sense the imposed melancholy of illicit love. Jack ordered a double brandy and the waiter smiled in condolence of what he could only assume. Jack asked if there was a table free out on the pavement terrace, and then moved outside. Sitting watching the passers by, he soon became distracted; absorbed in the mute theatre of their disparities. How many similar tragic stories to his were being played out daily in the anonymity of their existences, he wondered, or were most caught on the wheel of monotonous routine, fenced in the social corral of their mundane lives. He looked at his watch. Nearly two hours had passed, but he had time to kill; Lucy would not be returning to the hotel soon. He ordered a glass of red wine and a Croque Monsieur, recalling in his mind as he sunk into the perils of its deliciousness what he had said to Lucy only two days before: "I could do this every day."

Chapter 9

Pride Constrained

Lucy's father, Bernard, had been living in a small apartment in Tunbridge Wells for ten years by the time Jack's father died. It was a one bedroom, ground floor apartment with a through sitting/dining room large enough to accommodate his piano, close to The Pantiles where Lucy worked each morning, and within easy walking distance to a large super market. Soon after Joan's death, Bernard had felt increasingly ill at ease on his own in the house he had shared for so many years with her, despite the consolation of his beloved piano. Too many memories of their years together in the house, and images of her lifeless body lying on the bed emerged from the stillness, unsettling him whenever Lucy was not there to accompany him. Although she had talked about the possibility of Jack and her moving in with him, Bernard had not been keen on the idea. In his old age he valued his independence, he found comfort in the constancy of his routines, his way of managing; assisted by his daughter's daily visits. His idea at the time had been simply to sell the house on the open market, buy an apartment, and live for his remaining years on the monies provided by the difference. But Lucy had been loath to lose the family home of her childhood and had a better idea: she and Jack sold their house and bought her father's house; keeping the operation within the family so all had benefitted.

Jack and Lucy were down in Somerset for a long weekend break celebrating his fifty second birthday with Hugh and Belinda at the time he received the news of the death of his father Harold: visits that had become customary since their marriage and the births of Toby and Clara. They were sitting around the dining table, chatting, laughing and feeling mellow after a lunch of roast beef, apple crumble and a couple of bottles of Bordeaux. Jack was animated about the events then taking place in Europe. After weeks of watching the disintegration of Soviet satellite states on the television news – Poland, Czechoslovakia and Hungary – now the Berlin wall had finally fallen the previous week, and thousands of East Berliners had poured unhindered past the armed guards into West Berlin. In the euphoria of television chatter, much speculation of German unification filled the coverage dividing opinions. Jack, moved by the emotive sights of hard won freedom and families united was enthusiastically in favour, but Hugh was more sceptical, made wary by modern history, and concern of Germany's European domination. Sensing the snare of political confrontation, Hugh changed the subject to amusing reports of Toby's love life as he had heard it from the man himself, prompting Belinda laughingly to observe that he appeared to have taken more after his godfather than his real father. Lucy was keen to keep up to date on Clara's comings and goings. As her godmother, and not having children of her own to cherish, she had always paid special attention to Clara, they had become close over the years since she was a child, and she had encouraged Jack to do the same with Toby. That summer they had celebrated his twenty first birthday and he was now in his final year at the London School of Economics. Clara was up at Oxford taking modern languages and the history of art. Belinda said that after graduation, Clara wanted to go to Paris for a gap year so that she could perfect her spoken French. "She's not attracted to the idea of being an au pair like you did Lucy." Belinda explained. "If possible she would rather get an office job or work in a gallery. "Nearer the time," she said to Jack, "perhaps your sister's husband, Francois, could help her find a job."

The telephone call from Phyllis changed the mood instantly; silence fell as each considered the value of their consolation. Jack told his mother they would return home immediately, but Phyllis, ever practical, was calm and collected, assuring him there was no reason for them to rush back; there was little he could do that weekend. Jack knew Harold had been diagnosed with terminal prostate cancer some months before and given only months to live, like Hugh's father, so his passing at any time had been anticipated. But the sudden realisation that his father was gone for ever, that he would never again be there in his life, the pillar of his aspiration or resentment, left him deeply reflective with thoughts that had never entered his mind: his parents' generation were passing on, he would be the next, but then there would be none to mourn. He felt the need to get out into the garden, to breathe the cool air and put some longer visions to his mental focus.

"I don't think I would want to be told I only had so many months to live." Jack said to Hugh as they wandered over the lawns. "I know both our fathers were given expiry dates by their doctors, but knowing the inevitable must be the same inescapable mental agony as being on death row in prison. It's rather disconcerting that both our fathers died of the same bloody cause. I suppose it's a warning to both of us."

"Sad as it is we all have to die of something eventually." Hugh responded philosophically. I recall the doctor telling me at the time of my own father's diagnosis, that although some men die *of* prostate cancer, all men die *with* prostate cancer."

"That's not really very consoling Hugh." Jack responded

glumly. "The sadness is that despite knowing full well the inevitability of our parents' lives ending, somehow we are never really prepared for the absolute finality of death. We live our lives so occupied with the issues of every day, we don't allow ourselves time to consider more meaningful issues before suddenly it's all too late. We put those things on the back burner with the idea that we'll get around to it, but we don't. In that moment of ceasing to be, all that should have been said must have been said, and all that should not have been said cannot be retracted. In that second of death all tenses change: the present tense becomes the past and the future is gone for ever; all opportunities gone. Dad and I were so different. We didn't always agree - far from it - but somehow as he grew older and I grew a little wiser we came to understand each other better. I only wish now we could have talked more."

Following Phyllis's wishes Harold's funeral was kept strictly as a family affair, despite the numerous business friends he had made over the many years he had been at the top of his industry. The simple service was held in the small chapel of an isolated country graveyard overlooking a valley near the family home, where Harold's own father and mother had also been buried. It was the end of November, and although the last remnants of the warm weather that had lasted throughout the long summer had given way to the early morning frosts of winter, sunshine bathed the countryside. An elderly aunt, two uncles and a sprinkling of cousins attended. "Family I barely know of and have seldom, if ever, seen." Jack confided to Lucy; who brought her own father looking perilously close to joining Harold in everlasting peace. Hugh and Belinda came up from Somerset and Emily and her family dutifully came over from Paris: Francois now prematurely grey; Jules a slim, good looking young man; and Isabelle a vulnerably attractive young woman, chic in black Jack observed, and complemented her accordingly.

"I think if Dad had had a choice he would have opted for a sunny funeral." Jack suggested to Emily as they wandered away from the graveside. Always go out on a high. I can hear him say. On the other hand, however, one could imagine it being rather more comforting to be placed down in the earth on a grey, cold day…..you know, anything to escape the usual British climate." He chuckled at his own dark humour.

Emily appeared not to have heard her brother's inappropriate musings. "We have to get back to Paris in a couple of days Jack. Maybe while I'm over here we should try to have a chat with mum to see what she has in mind now that dad has gone."

"Don't you think it's a bit premature to try to speak with her about anything like that at the moment?" Jack responded. "She's never talked about her ideas of life after father's passing; you know, like the marital joke: when one of us dies I'm going to live in Switzerland." He chuckled. "Frankly she has always given me the impression that she'll jump off that bridge when she comes to it, as they say."

"Well you may be right, but nonetheless I think it's worth mentioning, even if it's only to trip her mind. The two of them rattling around in that big house may once have made some sense, but on her own I cannot see her staying there long. You know that for years dad's intention was for you to take over The Nunnery after he had gone. He wanted to establish a tradition and keep the property in the family; as he had done after his own father had died. I think he thought that in that way mum would be able to stay on in the house with you and Lucy taking care of her, you know, like Hugh and Belinda did with his mother."

"I really cannot see that happening for several reasons, not the least of which is that, unlike Hugh, I simply cannot and could not afford to maintain the property. Lucy and I are very happy where we are in her old family home; it's easily manageable and allows us to get away from time to time. The greater part of dad's capital will be in the value of The Nunnery, and I'm sure there will not be sufficient other funds to maintain the house and gardens in the long term. And of course there is another important factor to consider: Lucy and mother just don't get along. If we were going to try living together, I'm sure we would all soon be attending another funeral." He laughed ironically. "Frankly I think you should just be sweet to mother for the couple of days you're here, assure her that you would be there for her should she need you, and get back to Paris. In time I will get around to chatting it over with her, and I'll let you know her response." He said in a tone cynically anticipating that outcome.

Jack was on his own having tea with his mother at The Nunnery when he sensed the opportunity to raise the subject. It was already quite dark outside, and the crackle of the log fire in the large inglenook fireplace induced an aura of cosy invulnerability. Like many of his contemporaries, the ordered formality of customs he knew as a child had fallen by the wayside in the haste of modern life, but Phyllis stuck rigidly to the habits instilled in her early lifetime, and all the necessary ingredients for tea were carefully prepared and laid out on the trolley: finely cut bread and butter; jams; pastes; cucumber sandwiches; a newly baked Victoria sponge cake; and the silver tea pot with milk jug and sugar basin. With the care of the captain of a super tanker edging the colossal bulk of his vessel to quayside, Jack gradually brought the conversation around to the issue of his mother's plans for her future. But hardly had he uttered the gist of what he had in mind to say, when Phyllis made her thinking abundantly clear.

"If for one minute you and your sister think I would

leave this house, my advice would be to think again." She said firmly. "I suppose there are those that believe I should downsize now that I'm on my own, sell The Nunnery and buy a much smaller house, or that I would be better cared for living in a home for the elderly," she laughed at the thought, "but no, no it's out of the question. I want to remain here, and I will remain here until they take me out feet first."

"That's all very clear then." Jack responded briefly, while munching on a cucumber sandwich and imagining his mother's lifeless body horizontally elevated. "You don't think you could be a little lonely rattling around here on your own?"

"No dear I don't. Not as I feel now anyway." Phyllis said less stridently. "Like Bernard when Joan died, I greatly value my ability to be independent; when your time comes you'll understand." She said knowingly. "Here I have the comfort of the familiar around me every day. I can continue to potter about in the garden, pruning the roses and helping Henry the gardener. I think he was concerned about his job, but I have assured him I intend to plough on, and I have already spoken with Doreen about giving me more help. She has agreed to come now every morning and some afternoons if needs be; she's a cheery soul and good company. The thought of being cared for in a home appals me, although one day, who knows, I may be forced to change my mind."

"Well in many ways I do understand and I'm sure I

would feel exactly the same way. You're still pretty much on the ball mum, and I do think it's so important to keep busy, keep one's mind active, and this old house will certainly give you plenty of that to do as long as your monies last."

"Of course one could imagine in the present circumstances that it would have been easier for me if Emily had remained in England. But she's been happily married in Paris for years, and she has her own family to take care of. You know your father always had in mind that you would take over the house one day like he did when his father died. You and Emily will certainly be inheriting the property at some time anyway, and I'm sure you will sell it when the time comes. Emily has no need of it; her children are now grown up, and you and Lucy would not want it either."

When Jack returned home he felt the strange relief of a weight lifted he had not recognised until then he had been carrying since Emily had raised the question of his mother's future. His father had died - and that would leave a hole in his consciousness until time could heal the gap - but other than that, now that all was clear with his mother, he could not envisage any other problems to solve, or potential upheavals to disturb the contented order of his life. He reported back to Emily the decisiveness of their mother's plans for her future as she had clearly told him, and Emily said she was not surprised; she totally understood and would probably feel the same. She said that now that the children were pretty much off her hands, she would try to come over to England more frequently, and Jack should encourage her to visit Paris more often: "while she still retains her mental abilities and the energy to act on them." was how she put it.

Over the next couple of years Phyllis remained energetic and actively engaged in the house and garden as she had made clear her intention to do. She kept in touch with friends – most often other widows, inviting or being invited for tea - and occasionally joining forces with one or other to visit the Chelsea Flower Show, a National Trust property, or taking the morning train to London for a little shopping, lunch and an afternoon theatre. Encouraged by Jack she visited Emily, and each summer she took a cruise: once to the Norwegian fiords which she found "all rather the same – after one the rest get rather tedious," and once to the North African coast of the Mediterranean, finding

Leptis Magna "inspirational." Then intermittent lapses in her usual competence drew

Jack and Lucy's attention to the early signs of short term memory loss; dismissed by Phyllis with self deprecating humour. Unusually she might forget a hair appointment or to return a telephone call, and when speaking of a visit to Paris, she would at times refer to "Emily's husband" or "Emily's boy, or girl"; momentarily unable to recall their names.

Her stories were recounted jokingly to camouflage any

significance: "I went upstairs to my bedroom purposefully to get something or other, and when I got to the room, do you know, for the life of me I couldn't remember what I was doing there. The other day I forgot I had asked Sybil Thornton for lunch. When she arrived I had already eaten." She laughed heartily. "I had nothing else prepared, it was so embarrassing. I keep doing this these days." But short term loss appeared to be long term gain. With Harold now gone, Phyllis turned increasingly to nostalgic memories of their youthful years together: the thirties; the war years; the daily trials of rationing that followed; and her early years at The Nunnery remodelling the gardens.

In the early autumn of that year Clara started work in Paris. She had graduated well, and had taken a couple of months off during the summer to reacclimatise her mind from the concentrated focus of academic learning. Emily and Francois were more than happy to have her living with them: Jules (now a cub reporter with Le Canard enchaîné) had struck out and left home to live with his girl friend, and Clara was good company for Isabelle; still a fledgling reluctant to leave the nest. Only recently she had qualified as an architect, and been taken on by a fashionable young group practice with a number of exciting projects. Emily had gone back to working full time at Hachette in her old job as a proof reader checking typesetting. She had arranged a place for Clara as an assistant in her department: immersed all day in the language, she thought, was ideal for perfecting her written and spoken French; and a good way for Emily to keep an eye on her.

Clara and Isabelle got on well together; in their looks and temperaments they were two halves that somehow made a whole and soon they had become like sisters: Isabelle fair haired, blue eyed and self-effacing, and Clara black haired, brown eyed and self-assured. Clara was drawn to the gentleness of Isabelle's personality, and despite being the elder, Isabelle benefitted from Clara's confidence. Autumn's decline into the dismal days of winter dampened Clara's expectations of life in the city, but soon she was absorbed into the novelty of her work with Emily, and the stimulus of a small group of Isabelle friends from school and university with whom they met regularly: "a group that gets smaller each year as some get married and start families." Isabelle commented. The warm promises of spring gradually dispelled memories of the cold, grey chills of winter, and visions of the city's romanticism gradually re-emerged, like a bear emerges into the light from the dark slumber of its hibernation: fresh green leaves invigorated the trees on the boulevards; pavement cafés bustled with tourists and habitués engrossed in their daily newspapers; children with mothers pushed prams in the parks; and couples strolled hand in hand through the Tuileries gardens.

At dinner one evening Francois said that he had met

that day with one of the authors they published. He said he had been making small talk over lunch about Isabelle starting out on her career as an architect, and went on to mention Clara; saying that she was staying with them from England to get work experience, and perfect her French after graduating from Oxford. Apparently the man was interested because he has a daughter of more or less the same age as Clara, and hoped that the three young women could get together. "His daughter is going to do a summer course in Oxford this year, and he's anxious for her to practice her English as much as possible before she goes." Francois said. "You could also give her some helpful tips about Oxford Clara." He added.

"I think that's a nice idea." Clara said. "What do you think Isabelle?"

"Yes why not…..it's always good to meet new people. And maybe she has a handsome, mature older brother." She said with a feigned tone of optimistic anticipation. "The ones I knew for years in our group are all married off now. And those remaining I know too well." She added ironically.

"OK that's good." Francois said in conclusion. "I'll contact the guy and make some arrangement. Maybe the best idea is for you three young women to meet up in some place you all know one evening after work. I really don't think you need parents about at your ages; like some kids party." He laughed. Give me a place you'd like to meet, make it somewhere central, easy to find if she doesn't already know it."

"Le Ballon Rouge" in Rue Lafayette." Isabelle replied immediately. "She will very probably know it as it's a rather fashionable, groovy place where young meet up at the moment. It's easy to find anyway; opposite Gallerie Lafayette; about fifty metres or so up the street."

"Is there any particular day that's bad for either of you?"

Isabelle looked at Clara for confirmation. "No." They both said in unison.

"The Red Balloon. That was such a wonderful film." Emily said with yearning nostalgia. "Do you remember *chéri*; when we were first getting to know each other at university we went to see it together? I think it was the first time we held hands in the cinema." She giggled.

"Oooh naughty, naughty" Isabelle laughed. "What was the film about *Maman*?"

"It was rather a short little film I recall. I cannot remember the story entirely, but it's about this little boy who finds a huge red balloon on his way to school in Paris. The balloon becomes his friend with a personality of its own. It follows the little boy around like a pet. It was all beautifully filmed, but I think it ended sadly and I cried."

On the day and time Francois had arranged for the three young women to get together, Isabelle and Clara had positioned themselves at a table close to the entrance at Le

Ballon Rouge so as to be more easily noticed in the crowded café. They were happily singing along to 'Stars' - a hugely popular song by a group called 'Simply Red' – which was blaring out on the café's sound system. A tall, slim, leggy young blonde entered, looked around to identify the most likely people to fit a description she had been given, and confidently came over to their table.

"*Excusez-moi.* You are Isabelle and Clara?" She asked.

"Yes." The two girls said smiling broadly and rising to greet her."

"I'm sorry." Isabelle said. "Nobody has yet told us your name."

"My friends call me Leena." She said as they all sat down. A waitress came over spotting a new arrival and she ordered an Orangina.

"So Leena; you're going to Oxford this summer." Clara said by way of launching their conversation. "Maybe your father has already told you I was at the university. I took modern languages and the history of art. I came down early last summer."

In her manner, Leena exuded a maturity beyond her years contained in a gentle nature; attractive and seemingly unaware of her attractiveness. "Yes. I am going to Oxford at the end of June for four weeks to learn better my English. I also like to study the art history, but when I go to university here, I prefer to study *littérature et création littérataire.*

Perhaps you know my father is an *auteur* and I want to do the same."

As they sat chatting and Clara told Leena animatedly about her time at Oxford, gradually Isabelle found herself fading out of their conversation, her mind wandering into her job, plans she was working on, and a good looking young guy who appeared to be paying particular attention to her at the office. There was nothing she could say about Oxford, and lost in thought amongst the background din of piped music and Clara's chatter, for the first time she felt the significance in the difference in their ages: the liberty of her student days and attitudes were past, and she was now a qualified architect with a responsible job, she reminded herself. She reflected on the months Clara had been living with them and valued the close female companionship they had enjoyed together. But soon Clara would return to London to find her own path to independence, and she realised she must also leave home to do the same. After all, she thought, most of her friends were already married – some with children – it was ridiculous that she didn't have a regular boyfriend at her age; maybe she should get to know better the young man at the office.

Over the last few weeks of Clara's stay in Paris she made a point of seeing Leena regularly. They had become firm friends, and soon Clara's animated chatter became *their* animated chatter as Leena became much more confident and practiced in her English.

"When you book your flight tickets to London," Clara had pleaded, "please do make absolutely sure to add two more weeks onto the end of your trip to Oxford, so that you can come to stay with me at our home near Bath. I know my family, particularly my brother, would love to meet you," she laughed, "and you should see Bath anyway as a visitor to Britain – it's a beautiful city dating back to Roman times.

Isabelle did not join Clara and Leena again in their meetings, the sudden clarity of her self reflections during their first get-together had given her motivation to change her life, and she wanted to pursue those aims. She realised that for the past year since Clara had come to stay they had been inseparable; she had become a comfortable fixture in her life; her confidant in all she did and thought, and perhaps for that reason, she had had no incentive to reflect on the lack of direction in her personal life. Now that Clara would soon be leaving to return to England, maybe it was not a bad thing for them to be seeing less of each other, she thought, in preparation for that break. Her prime concern was for

Emily. It was clear her mother had enjoyed the motherliness of having Clara to take care of, both at home and at her office, and with her gone, and she herself also striking out for her own independence, it would surely leave a gapping hole in her mother's life. If she broke the news gently now, it might reduce the impact when the time arrived.

"After Clara returns to England *maman*, I think the time has come for me also to leave the nest." She said while helping to prepare their evening meal in the kitchen. "I can't stay at home for the rest of my life – it's unhealthy," she laughed to lighten the message. "If Clara hadn't come to stay with us, maybe I would have moved out before. But I've so enjoyed having her company for this last year, I haven't thought about getting on with it."

"I think that would be a very good idea *chérie*. You've got a good job and a bright future ahead; you should now be independent."

"Oh." Isabelle said with disappointed surprise. "Do you want me to leave? I thought you'd be depressed at the thought of being alone."

"No....." Emily said warmly hastening across to give her daughter a hug of love and assurance, "don't be silly *chérie*. Of course daddy and I will miss you, and of course we don't want you to leave, but we know you should and must leave home to be independent and start your own life: meet the right man, marry, have children of your own and be happy like your father and I. The one gift all parents can give their children is their independence and the ability to be independent. It's wrong to want to cling on."

"Won't you be lonely with us two girls gone?"

"Of course it'll be strange to begin with, but I'm sure daddy and I will start travelling a bit more, finding our new lives together, and you'll be visiting us regularly anyway; even if it's only to get your laundry done." She laughed.

"I've been looking at advertisements for apartments to rent in the newspapers for the last few weeks; just to get an idea of prices in the various *arrondissements*. I haven't been to see anything as I really would like your advice. After Clara has gone maybe you and daddy could help me; we could go to see some places together. I would like to try to find somewhere as close as possible to my office, or on a direct Metro line anyway."

On the Saturday of Clara's departure an air of melancholy pervaded the apartment; mute recognition for the ending of a phase and vague uncertainty as to what lay ahead. Breakfast conversation was of happy memories recalled, with gratitude for all that had been given, and promises of reunions to come. Time hung heavily with each participant begrudging its passing, yet unable fully to exploit the steadily depleting value of its present; paradoxically despondent at the thought of the impending separation, yet anxious to get past the pain of parting. While Clara packed her bag, Francois read the newspaper, Isabelle retired to her room and Emily busied herself in the kitchen. During all the months of her stay, while Clara had been a valuable friend for Isabelle, she knew she would miss her company the most. They had spent so many hours each day together, and she had grown close to Clara in a motherly way, caring for her at home and at the office, where she had seen her blossom in her time from a competent adolescent to a street wise young woman. Unexpectedly Jules turned up to say goodbye with regrets that they had not seen each other more often, and Leena telephoned to wish her luck and confirm the dates of her stay after finishing her summer course. At the airport they stood and watched as Clara passed through passport control. She turned to wave goodbye; she was going home so she had all that to look forward to, she said to herself, but she had tears in her eyes for all the love she was leaving behind.

Over the first few weeks following her return from Paris Clara was unsettled. Outwardly she was happy to be home with her family in the familiar surroundings of her childhood, but a curious underlying nostalgia, a strange homesickness lurked in her inner consciousness for the newly found life she had left behind: the cosmopolitan buzz of the beautiful, historic city, the self recompense of conversing in a newly acquired language with newly acquired friends, and the pleasures of discovery by immersion in the culture of a foreign land. Looking out over the gardens from the window of her bedroom, grey clouds filled the sky crowding small patches of blue. A passing rain shower fell on the kaleidoscopic array of flowers in bloom, and a tinge of depression weighed on her mind: it was early summer and she was back in England with the mundane Englishness of her English country life. She knew that by the autumn she must find a job, a stimulating job in which she could make advantage of her qualifications and fluent French. Having worked with Hachette in Paris (and with a little help from Francois) she was confident of finding a job with one of their publishing houses in London. But a perceived self image of a life immersed in the beauty of fine art and antiques, with an authoritative knowledge of that world gleaned over time, drew her towards a career with a leading auction house. A faint childhood memory percolated into her mind that her father's uncle – a prominent merchant banker – had been on the Board of Directors of Christie's before his retirement. "Interesting" she said to herself, keen to pull every string to get the right introduction, she would pursue that possibility, and spend the next few weeks in the greater stimulus of London with her brother Toby, before Leena came to stay.

Six months after leaving the London School of Economics, Toby had been taken on by Cazenove & C° in the City with whom his father, Hugh, had been working before joining his father's stock broking partnership in Bath. He was living in the comparative luxury of the family flat in Beaufort Gardens: too comfortably convenient to ignore while he professed to be looking for a place of his own. Ownership of the property had been passed to Belinda by her father a couple of years previously in a gamble to reduce death duties. On graduating Toby had taken a few months travelling around Spain to relish the exhilaration of freedom before settling into work. After picking up the pilgrimage route in Toulouse, he hiked over the Pyrenees mountains to Santiago de Compostela, then making his way by road and rail southward through Extremadura, east to Cordoba and Granada, north to Toledo and ending in Madrid. Travelling light, engaging with locals and awed by the sun baked panorama of endless landscapes, he became enraptured with the country steeped in ancient traditions, and the blood soaked bravura of its history. He wallowed in his liberty from the shackles of dictated routine, the romantic ideal of a life free of constraints, and struggled with the rationality of submitting himself again to the drudgery of a daily job and the established orders of custom. Increasingly the voice of an inner devil wormed its way into his thoughts urging him to rebel, but rebellion is tough in the face of instilled disciplines and a limited budget. Reluctantly he returned home.

Toby and Clara had been close as brother and sister since childhood, and in their late adolescence, Toby had relished the bounteous bevy of Clara's nubile girl friends who regularly frequented their home. Tall, dark, athletic and broodingly introspective, at university he had been a magnet for the attentions of attractive young women of a motherly nature; and others that others would have been more than happy to know. He remained purposefully unattached, enjoying the company of women, and loosening the ties of any relationship at the first hint of entrapment. He was happy to have Clara with him in London at the flat: in the short period between his return from Spain and her departure for Paris, they had not found time to 'hang out' together, and now they had so much to tell, stories to recount and impressions to relate. Clara was intrigued by his colourful adventures in Spain; imagining the colour and heat of each scene as he spoke, poring over the pile of photos, and relating personally to his reluctance to return; noting to visit as soon as she was able. By contrast, recollections of her stay in Paris working could not carry the same vibrancy. He empathised with her current inability to readjust to life back home, assuring her unconvincingly it would diminish over time. A glimmer of increased interest registered on the mention of Leena and her forthcoming visit. "She sounds divine from your enthusiastic description. When did you say she was coming? I'll have to make a large note in my diary to coincide my holidays with that time."

Pursuing her aim through her contacts, Clara secured a job interview at Christie's. After a second interview and an anxious period of waiting - eagerly checking the post each day - a letter arrived with good news: she had been accepted as a trainee to start conveniently on the first Monday of September. Initially her interviewer suggested Clara join their intern programme, "to get an overall feeling of the business, see if the actuality of the work meets the glamour of your imagination." was how she had expressed it. But Clara was insistent, emphasising her degree course, her long held love of antiques and fluent French: this was the career she saw for herself, with a learning that would give a constant gratification for a lifetime.

When Leena called to make contact in the last week of her summer course Clara was chirpy. She could relax knowing she had a good job to look forward to, and the summer free to enjoy. "It's so good to hear from you again," she said enthusiastically,

"You must tell me all about your time in Oxford when you come. I have a good job now starting in September. I'll tell you all about it when I see you. When you know the time you will be arriving by train into London on Friday, let me know and I'll meet you at Paddington station. Our train to Bath leaves from the same station which is useful."

When the two young women arrived at Bath Spa, Hugh was there to collect them at the station. Following her return from Paris, he had heard a lot about Leena from his daughter, and on meeting her he could see and sense the attraction of opposites that had drawn them close as friends. On the way home, Clara sat next to her father chattering endlessly of her new job, what she had been up to in London, and pointing out features of the countryside as they passed. Leena sat meditatively silent in the back absorbing all.

The next morning Toby arrived unexpectedly. He had driven down from London on a whim having previously registered with his company from an obscure entry in his diary that he would be taking two weeks holiday at this time. Clara was joyous to see him, rushing out to greet him on seeing the arrival of his car. "You remembered." She exclaimed excitedly. "Remembered what?" He asked, instantly knowing the answer as Leena emerged from the house.

"Hi I'm Toby." he said extending his hand in greeting as they came together. "I suppose it's rather fatuous to say I've heard so much about you from Clara, but maybe you're already aware how she goes on about anything or anybody she finds attractive." He chuckled.

Leena automatically leaned towards him to kiss and embrace in the insignificant manner of French etiquette, but instantly withdrew now aware of the absence of such physicality in English custom. "Yes." She replied sweetly with a twinkle in her eye. "I have heard a lot about you too." She laughed gently.

"Don't you just love that soft French accent on the English language?" Toby remarked to Clara.

Leena looked coyly self aware and a pregnant silence hung frozen in the air as if time had momentarily stopped: a metaphysical recognition, an indefinable awareness that something meaningful had sparked between two people meeting for the first time.

On hearing Clara's welcome and chatter in the driveway, Belinda came out to see who had caused the excitement. "Oh hello darling," she said on seeing Toby, wiping her hands on her apron and giving him a motherly embrace, "I'm just preparing lunch. We weren't expecting you this weekend were we?"

"No I must apologise." Toby responded. "I do hope you're not overbooked." He laughed. Actually you've got me for the whole week at least, maybe more, I trust that's not inconvenient. I found this semi legible note in my diary: Take holiday, followed by a scribble. Frankly I couldn't remember making the entry or why, but the curtness of the note appeared so compelling, I thought I should comply. Now I'm here, and looking around," he added flirtingly, "I'm really rather glad I did."

Through each day of the following week it was subtly becoming clear to all the degree to which Toby and Leena were attracted to each other. They were conspicuously inseparable, not outwardly wanting to appear so by the pretence of their actions, although awkwardly aware that maybe they were, but unable to resist the underlying desire.

Leena appeared aware of the hurt she may be causing Clara, purposefully involving her at all times, drawing her close to allay any feelings of alienation. Imagining this visit when she had first mentioned the idea to Leena in Paris, Clara had envisaged the two of them enjoying girlie days in the countryside and in Bath shopping, with herself as guide to the city's historic sites. But it was all turning out so differently and she was confused. This was a very different Toby. Not the Toby of reputation. Yes she had been keen for them to meet and was happy they got on well and would do nothing to unsettle that, but now there were too many times she felt self consciously superfluous; an intruder in their involvement, and she had to fight back tinges of jealousy. After all, she said to herself naively, Leena was primarily her friend.

By the end of the week it was clear that Toby and Leena were very much in love. They had toured around the many beauty spots of the area, involving Clara in their plans for each day, but short periods of sunshine interspersed with bouts of rain dampened enthusiasm for country activities. Leena mentioned to Toby the possibility of visiting London; she said she had only passed through on her way to Oxford, and maybe he and Clara could show her around. Toby thought that was a great idea, and when he told his mother that Leena would come with him and Clara to London for her last week before flying back to Paris, Belinda knew where this was heading, but instinctively said little. She valued the close relationship she enjoyed with her son, and would not allow herself to interfere in his private life. Naturally she recognised that she had a responsibility for Leena as a guest in her house, but Leena was a mature young woman of twenty years of age who could not be told what to do; no longer a child requiring motherly protection. Having noted the speedy intensity of the Toby's relationship with Leena, and taking advantage of a convenient moment alone with his son, Hugh gave the fatherly advice he had once given Jack: be responsible; be respectful; think it through carefully; and do not rush into anything. Before leaving for London, Toby took Clara aside and expressed to her as best he could the strength of his feelings for Leena. He explained that he had never experienced such an attraction before, this was not a self interested flirtation he assured her, and hoped that she would understand: he was not taking Leena's friendship from her but bringing it closer, more personal, perhaps even more permanent.

"So in that case then, wouldn't it be undiplomatic of me to come back with you to London? I really don't want to find myself a spare prick at the wedding, or whatever the female equivalent of that is." She giggled.

"No of course we want you to come; don't be daft. It's only natural Leena would feel better with you around." Toby said convincingly, giving his sister a big hug.

Before they all left, Clara went to Leena's room while she was preparing her suitcase, admiring the meticulous order in which she was packing her clothes. "Well this has all turned out rather unexpectedly." She said affectionately. "Please don't feel badly about it though, I'm really happy for you both, and excited by the thought of how it may all turn out." She continued in a manner conveying a question with a predetermined answer. "I wanted you to meet Toby, I knew you'd get on well, I just didn't envisage you both falling in love so quickly: silly me." She laughed.

Leena came away from the bed. "Oh Clara thank you for being so sweet, but I do feel bad." She said hugging her tightly. "I know you planned this visit would be just our two weeks together, but nobody knows what life has in store. Now we will have to see what the future holds. Anyway, I will go back to Paris as planned. I will be starting at the university in the autumn."

Clara pulled a sad face. "I'm sure Toby will be heartbroken poor chap. Anyway we have got all the week to be together in London before you leave; it'll be fun. After that we can keep in touch regularly. I'm certain to be visiting my aunt Emily at every possible opportunity, and meanwhile I have an exciting job to start."

Arriving at the flat in London, an unspoken presumption hung in the air, but no question was raised: Toby went to his room and Leena automatically followed

Clara to hers. With little food in the fridge and shops closed on Sunday, they settled on pizza at a nearby restaurant, watched television and went to bed. On waking the next morning Clara was surprised to find Leena still in the bed next to hers. Not because she had forgotten where she was and why she was there, but because she had expected Leena would not be. In the privacy of their girls' talk, neither had mentioned the more personal, more physical aspect of love, and like the recognition of the inevitable before the arrival of the actuality, a curious atmosphere of anticipation pervaded.

With each day together, Toby and Leena grew closer through shared confidences and the increased intimacy of their relationship. Tactfully Clara often pleaded other arrangements allowing them to be alone, and on the third morning of her stay when she woke, Leena was not in bed. Clara supposed she was in the bathroom, but when she did not return to the room and Clara checked, she was not there. A smile of gender unanimity crossed her face as the realisation of where she was entered her mind: "Yes." She said decisively in a mute tone of accomplishment. "That's my girl."

Although in her mind she had recognised its probability, Leena had been hesitant to make love, concerned that her time with Toby had been too short to know each other so intimately, without the benefit of a shared past to know each other better. She was not a virgin - she had been in an intimate relationship before she had met Clara in Paris - and the hurt and humiliation of that failed relationship had left her wary. She knew he knew she was returning to Paris at the end of the week, and an inner disquiet questioned the longer term seriousness of his intentions. He was good looking with an easy, flirtatious manner, the sort of young man who would attract a string of girlfriends: why would he settle on me she kept asking herself? She was concerned of getting too emotionally involved and too deeply committed; if there was little possibility of a future together.

But soon these concerns had evaporated in the thoughtfulness of Toby's affection, and the expressed certainty of his love: his talk of commitment; of their futures together; his anxiety to keep contact and visit each other frequently. She was deeply in love, and by the day of her return flight to Paris, the thought of her leaving was a dull ache for both to endure. While Leena packed her suitcase, striving to maintain her composure, be adult and not cave in to the yearning temptation to stay like a love sick adolescent, Toby busied himself needlessly about the apartment, dreading the inevitability of a predetermined mandate over which he had had no knowledge or voice. With the car packed up for the drive to the airport, he stood by nervously as Clara hugged Leena in the street; tearfully caught up in the emotions of the moment, and mutual empathy for the suppressed, stomach churning emotions of their pain. Clara waved until the car disappeared from view then went upstairs and quietly sobbed: homesick in her own home.

At the airport Toby parked the car and they walked purposefully to the terminal, each inwardly aware every step was a step towards the inevitable. After checking in Toby suggested they have a coffee before she went through to the departure area, but Leena was not keen saying "please let's not make this any more difficult." So much had been said in the days and hours before this moment, there was little more to add that might make their separation more bearable. Toby stood and watched as she walked through to the security check, an image in his mind praying that she would turn and rush back into his arms as they did in old Hollywood films. She didn't and was gone.

Over the next two years Toby and Leena kept in touch by telephone almost daily and visited each other regularly, like a married couple separated by the inconvenience of them both having irresistibly remunerative jobs in two different cities. Toby had the convenience of Emily's home to stay where he was always welcome whenever he could pop over to Paris for a weekend, and often during her breaks from the university, Leena came to stay with him in London. Although he had basic schoolboy knowledge of French, Toby was keen to get a better grasp of the language, become more conversationally fluent like his sister, in order to understand and participate more easily whenever with family and friends in France. He asked Clara to coach him in the evenings whenever convenient, and soon he was surprised at how quickly elements of

Learning, long since unused, returned to his mind. Some evenings they agreed to converse only in French, and soon Leena was joking that she must now be more careful what she said in front of him; Toby understood all.

When at last Leena completed her studies, Toby lost no time in proposing marriage: having patiently survived through the periodic vacuum of nocturnal doubts and demonic temptations denied for so long, he was anxious to reach a more settled state. Leena instantly accepted, and an approximate date was agreed for early that summer. Hugh and Belinda were thrilled when they heard the news. Since they had first met Leena they had been fully supportive of their son's attraction to her, and in many ways she had already become an established member of their family. Since being at Christie's, Clara also appeared to have found a serious new love with a young man named Jamie she had met working in the Oriental department: already Belinda could happily perceive the arrival of grandchildren re-animating the vacant corridors of her home.

Jack was surprised when his secretary informed him that a Mrs. Henderson was waiting for him in Reception;

for a brief moment he puzzled over the name.

"Mrs Henderson. How are you? What a nice surprise." He said in a formal manner with a twinkle in his eye as he approached Belinda. "What brings you up to town?"

Belinda looked baffled at the pantomime. "Why the Mrs. Henderson bit? Are we concealing something here?" She asked with a laugh, peering around with feigned concern looking for hidden cameras.

"My secretary informed me that a Mrs. Henderson was waiting for me in Reception, and do you know," he chuckled, "for a minute I wondered who the hell is that? I'm not used to Mrs. Henderson, I think of you as Belinda."

"Actually I popped in to use your loo." She laughed.

"A pee before me?" Jack asked with mock indignation.

"No seriously, I was in the area as I'm meeting Leena's mother for lunch at Langan's to chat about the up coming wedding. I thought you might like to join us so you can meet her, you know, being Toby's godfather and all. Are you free for lunch?"

"Well that all sounds very nice. Actually I did have a lunch date, but the fellow called earlier to push it over to tomorrow so yes, I would love to join you."

They strolled down Bond Street and crossed over through Berkeley Square to Stratton Street. The restaurant was packed and buzzing with the lunchtime diners as they entered; Belinda looked around to see if there was a lonely figure waiting at the bar or a table, but there was not. The maître d' showed them to a round table on the side, and Belinda explained that they expected another woman to join them, and would he please direct her to their table when she arrived.

"Hugh and I went over to Paris last month to meet Leena's mother to discuss Toby's upcoming wedding." Belinda said as a waiter busied himself around their table.

"She's a very nice woman; I think you'll like her. She and I discovered in conversation that both our grandmothers came from Carpentra. Actually she looks a little like me, now that I come to think of it. She too has black hair, dark eyes, olive skin and the same shaped nose; although she's a little taller than I am."

"Ah." Jack chuckled. "Maybe one of your two grandfathers was promiscuous."

Belinda smiled. "Well anything's possible I suppose. Anyway, we went to Paris to make a proposal. As Leena has been to stay with us a couple of times or so, and if she agreed to be married in England, we offered to have the wedding reception in a marquee in the garden at our home. In summer Paris can be awful; the locals flood out and the tourists flood in. Somehow it just seemed easier to have a country wedding, which is finally what we all agreed to. I got the impression that they're not particularly wealthy," she said in a conspiratorial tone, "so for us to pick up the costs of the reception was possibly rather welcome."

At that moment, Jack's attention was drawn to a woman nearing their table, and a jab of adrenalin instantly burned deep in his stomach, a dull ache constricted his chest: it was Anouk and neither had time to prepare. Belinda looked up saying by way of a greeting, "Oh wonderful, you made it Anouk. May I introduce you to Jack Strange; Jack is Toby's godfather."

Placing his napkin carefully on the table to allow a fraction more time to compose himself, Jack eased back his chair and stood to greet Anouk. "How do you do, it's a great pleasure to meet you." he said, extending his hand to shake hers and smiling broadly; praying her theatrical ability matched his own.

"It's a pleasure to meet you too." She responded looking him straight in the eyes with no hint of recognition before taking her seat. "I'm sorry if I'm a bit late. I took the metro to Green Park thinking it would be quicker than a taxi with all the traffic, but maybe I was wrong."

Relieved that no sign on either's part could have betrayed their secret up to that point, Jack relaxed. A déjà vu image flashed across his mind as Anouk explained the reason for her late arrival: she had said something very similar at Les Deux Magots the last time they met fifteen or so years ago.

As the two women talked of Paris, families and

wedding plans, Jack wondered why Belinda had asked him to come. Surely she would have realised that he would have little to add to such a conversation. Maybe somehow their secret was known, and this was a ploy to drag it out into the open, or was this fate once again demonstrating its Machiavellian mischief. The thought occurred to him that the risk of a fatal mistake must lie in direct proportion to the amount spoken, and cautioned himself from appearing too familiar with someone who, in theory, he had only just met. For once he decided that the best strategy was to say as little as possible. Smiling and appearing to be involved with their conversation he furtively studied Anouk. The youthful beauty of her slim, lithe body, shiny black hair, silken olive skin and chic femininity that he had found so irresistible in her younger years, had inevitably been dissolved by the demands of time. She was fuller in the face and figure now; her hair less lustrous and skin less silken portraying a more sensual womanliness gleaned through life's experiences. He recalled how they had then been together; the carefree, zestful energy of their youthful love. In his mind's eye he saw himself still as he was then: only mirrors negated that self deception. He glanced at the two women chatting and smiled to himself: by seeing Belinda regularly, he realised he had paid little close attention to her in the way he was now with Anouk. Familiarity conceals changes more easily noticed in friends one sees rarely, he concluded; and to think I was once clandestine lovers with both of them.

"So why does she call herself Leena and not Jacqueline?" Jack heard Belinda ask, bringing him out of his reverie. It was a question he had himself been tempted to ask, but was concerned it may inadvertently indicate some prior involvement.

"There was another Jacqueline in the same class with her at school." Anouk explained. "They decided that one would be Leena to make life easier. I suppose she got used to it and it stuck."

"I must say Leena is unusual." Jack said, purposefully stressing 'unusual'. It's a pity though, for me Jacqueline is so much prettier, more feminine don't you agree? I think I will call her Jacqueline from now, who knows, maybe it will catch on."

When the conversation began to slow, Jack said he must be getting back to the office; Belinda said she was going to pop down St. James's to see Clara; and Anouk said she was hoping to be having supper with Toby that evening. On the pavement outside,

Jack held back as Belinda and Anouk kissed their goodbyes, promising to keep in touch regularly. As Anouk then stepped towards Jack, each could sense through the eyes of the other the inner turmoil that had lain comfortably dormant for so many years. For her this was no longer a matter of her daughter marrying a young Englishman, nor

for him his godson a pretty French girl. Now *i.*
was to marry his godson - in other circumstanc
occasion - but in this case mined with potential
Jack took her two arms in his hands and gave her
on each cheek in the French style. "I'm sure as the br
mother you must be worrying about a hundred and on
things for your daughter's happiness." He said. "But you
really must not worry; my godson is a terrific guy. I'm
very happy Toby and Jacqueline found each other." Anouk
smiled and thanked him for his kindness, then turned and
walked up the street into Piccadilly.

"Well that was very sweet of you." Belinda commented.
"You were rather quiet over lunch though, not your usual
chatty self." She paused contemplating whether to continue.
"Actually, I have to say, when Anouk first came to our table
and you stood to say hello, I couldn't help noticing a strange
something in the air between you two; as if you had met
before." She said smiling knowingly at Jack in anticipation
of an admission.

"Maybe we have, but it must have been in another
life." Jack said dismissively. No I can assure you we haven't.
She's an attractive woman: perhaps what registered on my
facial expression was because, as you said before, you are
very much alike, you could be closely related; who knows,
perhaps you are." He laughed.

After much cross Channel communication, the

...aturday 16th of July. On the day

...dark blue sky, it was hot, and while

...e humidity with a wild profusion of

...ens, and the women present enjoyed the

...light summer outfits, the men suffered,

...formal morning suits with waistcoats.

...d Lucy had driven down earlier in the week,

...with Hugh and Belinda as usual in order to help with all the last minute arrangements to be made, and matters to be checked. A large marquee had been erected on the lawn as a precaution against the vagaries of the English summer; with its covering now providing much needed shade, and sides open to allow a welcome breeze to flow through. Down one side a long table bedecked with flowers held centre stage for the bride and groom and close members of their respective families. At one end of the marquee was an open buffet, and a bar and small dance floor at the other. A host of round tables and chairs occupied the space in the middle, with glorious flower arrangements on pedestals decorating each corner.

After the service guests filtered back from the church; friends finding each other and forming groups as they percolated through the gardens into the marquee and settled at tables. Catering staff moved amongst them offering a selection of drinks and eats. Gradually the level of conversation rose as the marquee filled; a mixed babble of French and English divided by the familiar comfort of language. Everyone agreed the central couple looked a perfect match: the groom tall, dark and handsome, the bride radiantly beautiful; her tall, slim figure elegantly sheathed in simple white silk, her long blonde hair swept up into a large bun at the back, decorated with tiny white flowers accentuating her femininity.

Mingling before seating, Lucy saw Clara and Isabelle talking animatedly with Leena. "Look at those three girls." She said to Jack drawing his attention. "Somehow it's so rewarding to see them so intensely involved as young friends. If we had had the good fortune to have children, I would have loved to have had three daughters; even if it would have meant paying for three weddings." she laughed light heartedly to lighten the message.

Jack did not respond; it had been a long time since that subject had risen. He too had been looking at Jacqueline, and suffering inwardly with different thoughts. She was so beautiful and he was proud, but it was a fatherly pride he could never share. Fate had given him a daughter, the daughter that Lucy had so craved. How desperately he wished life could have been different; he had loved her since almost the first moment they met.

Their marriage was a happy marriage of lovers and best friends. They had been a good team, successful in most of what they had set out to achieve, but childlessness had left a hole in their lives, accentuated on occasions such as this.

To the raucous delight of the French contingent, in his speech Toby broke fluently into their language. He said he recognised that by marrying Leena he stood accused of having stolen one of their national treasures, but asked them in turn, in the spirit of *entente cordiale*, to accept now her importance to both countries, promising to share her presence as equally as possible in future years. When all the speeches were over, and champagne toasts to the bride and groom had further elevated the party spirit, the music started. Following tradition, Toby and Leena took to the floor in a slow, romantic waltz, soon joined by Clara and Jamie; Isabelle and Jean Paul (the handsome young architect at her office); Jules and his girl friend Claudette; and then by a frenzy of the younger guests as the beat turned to disco. Jack and Lucy went over to Hugh and Belinda who were talking with Anouk and Gilles. They had met briefly earlier in the day at the church, but Anouk appeared to have been keeping her distance.

"What a truly wonderful wedding." Lucy commented.

"Thank you." Hugh said. "And aren't we lucky for such a glorious day?"

"You have met Anouk and Gilles, Leena's parents, haven't you?" Belinda asked. "Or should I say Jacqueline's parents." She hastily added, looking at Jack for acknowledgement that she had recalled his comment. "I know you have already met

Anouk – I well remember your insistence on 'Jacqueline' at our lunch at Langan's."

"Yes. We met briefly at the church." Jack replied turning directly to Gilles. "I'm sorry I didn't then have an opportunity to congratulate you." He continued. "I must say, you have a very beautiful daughter. You must be very proud."

An enigmatic smile lingered on Anouk's face: perceived gratitude and admiration for the superficial sincerity of Jack's theatrical performance, and the hidden contentment of a more profound satisfaction.

"Well shall we go and show those kids how to jive properly?" Jack chirpily said to Lucy, taking her hand and pulling her towards the dance floor.

"Oh God, here we go again; making a bloody fool of himself." Lucy responded with mock despair.

As they made their way to the floor Lucy commented to Jack conspiratorially. "I must say, now that we've met Anouk and Gilles, it's a little strange, don't you think, that Jacqueline is so tall and blonde? I mean, they're both so dark and sort of medium height. It must be a throw back to an earlier family gene on his side or hers I suppose. She's not an orphan is she?" She asked rhetorically. "Silly me, how would you know. Of course there could be another answer." She chuckled. "It happens in the best of families."

Printed in Great Britain
by Amazon

21011401R00161